This mo
ROUND-THE-CLOC
by Michelle

Nita Windcroft doesn't need a live-in bodyguard,
but she can't resist him. While they work together
to find the vandal wreaking destruction on her
land, she finds more and more to like about
Connor Thorne. Nita knows he wants her,
but the stubborn man won't give in!

**SILHOUETTE DESIRE
IS PROUD TO PRESENT**

A new drama unfolds for six of the state's
wealthiest bachelors.

* * *

And don't miss the next installments of the
TEXAS CATTLEMAN'S CLUB:
THE SECRET DIARY series

HIGHLY COMPROMISED POSITION
by Sara Orwig
November 2005

and

A MOST SHOCKING REVELATION
by Kristi Gold
December 2005

Available from Silhouette Desire!

Dear Reader,

Sit back, relax and indulge yourself with all the fabulous offerings from Silhouette Desire this October. Roxanne St. Claire is penning the latest DYNASTIES: THE ASHTONS with *The Highest Bidder.* Youngest Ashton sibling, Paige, finds herself participating in a bachelorette auction and being "won" by a sexy stranger. Strangers also make great protectors, as demonstrated by Annette Broadrick in *Danger Becomes You,* her most recent CRENSHAWS OF TEXAS title.

Speaking of protectors, Michelle Celmer's heroine in *Round-the-Clock Temptation* gets a bodyguard of her very own: a member of the TEXAS CATTLEMAN'S CLUB. Linda Conrad wraps up her miniseries THE GYPSY INHERITANCE with *A Scandalous Melody.* Will this mysterious music box bring together two lonely hearts? For something a little darker, why not try *Secret Nights at Nine Oaks* by Amy J. Fetzer? A handsome recluse, an antebellum mansion—two great reasons to stay indoors. And be sure to catch Heidi Betts's *When the Lights Go Down,* the story of a plain-Jane librarian out to make some serious changes in her humdrum love life.

As you can see, Silhouette Desire has lots of great stories for you to enjoy. So spend this first month of autumn cuddled up with a good book—and come back next month for even more fabulous reads.

Enjoy!

Melissa Jeglinski

Melissa Jeglinski
Senior Editor
Silhouette Desire

Please address questions and book requests to:
Silhouette Reader Service
U.S.: 3010 Walden Ave., P.O. Box 1325, Buffalo, NY 14269
Canadian: P.O. Box 609, Fort Erie, Ont. L2A 5X3

ROUND-THE-CLOCK *Temptation*

MICHELLE CELMER

Published by Silhouette Books

America's Publisher of Contemporary Romance

Special thanks and acknowledgement are given to Michelle Celmer for her contribution to the TEXAS CATTLEMAN'S CLUB: THE SECRET DIARY series.

 SILHOUETTE BOOKS

ISBN 0-373-76683-1

ROUND-THE-CLOCK TEMPTATION

Visit Silhouette Books at www.eHarlequin.com

Printed in U.S.A.

Books by Michelle Celmer

Silhouette Desire

Playing by the Baby Rules #1566
The Seduction Request #1626
Bedroom Secrets #1656
Round-the-Clock Temptation #1683

Silhouette Intimate Moments

Running on Empty #1342

MICHELLE CELMER

lives in southeastern Michigan with her husband, their three children, two dogs and two cats. When she's not writing or busy being a mom, you can find her in the garden or curled up with a romance novel. And if you twist her arm real hard you can usually persuade her into a day of power shopping.

Michelle loves to hear from readers. Visit her Web site at: www.michellecelmer.com, or write her at P.O. Box 300, Clawson, MI 48017.

To Melissa Jeglinski, for taking an eight-year dream and making it a reality. Words cannot express my gratitude.

To Patience Smith, for being the editor I had always dreamed of and then some, and her unwavering faith in me. It has truly been a joy to work with you.

To my agent, Jessica Faust, for her unconditional support, for talking me down from the ledge a time or two and for being a hell of a lot of fun (and of course perky).

To the exceptional authors I had the privilege of getting to know while working on this project. Cindy, Brenda, Shirley, Sara and Kristi, thanks for making my first continuity such a fun, rewarding experience.

To Wanda Ottewell for diving into this midproject and managing to make sense of it all. I'd love to work with you again.

And finally, to my brother and sister-in-law, Jim and Sue, for their help researching this book. Thanks, guys!

Prologue

*From the diary of Jessamine Golden
October 11, 1910*

Dear Diary

Just when I thought I'd lost my taste for revenge,
when I believed Brad's love for me had lifted the
dark shadows that hung over my heart, I've been
betrayed once again. Edgar Halifax stole my family and my security when he murdered my father.
He ruined my life and took away my dreams of
being a teacher. Now he's stolen the only man I
could ever love, the only man who has ever loved
me, and my thirst for revenge is like a fire burning out of control in my belly.

I've been framed, Diary. I didn't steal that gold

and I told Brad so. I swore to him on my father's grave that it wasn't me, that it was Halifax himself who'd done it. That he'd taken the gold and hidden it and made it look like a robbery. But Diary, when I saw the doubt in Brad's eyes I felt sick deep inside my soul and a sharp pain stole my breath. It was my heart ripping in two. I've been betrayed before, but it never hurt like this. I realize now what a fool I've been to let myself believe we could beat the odds.

But, Lord, I still love him. I crave the lips that touched mine so sweetly, the hands that caressed me so tenderly. The pendant rests close to my heart, a reminder of all that could have been. I'll keep it there, even though I know now our love can never be. In Brad's heart he will forever be a man of the law and my thirst for revenge will never be quenched. Not until Halifax pays for his sins. And he will pay. I'll see to that.

Without Brad's love, I have nothing left to lose.

One

Nita Windcroft wasn't the crying sort.

The last time she'd shed a tear had been thirteen years ago, in the fourth grade, when she fell off the monkey bars and dislocated her shoulder. Buck Johnson had laughed and called her a baby and she'd hauled off and given him a black eye with her good arm. As far as she was concerned, most females were way too emotional for their own good. But in light of the recent happenings at their family horse farm—deliberately broken fences, poisoned feed that nearly killed more than a dozen horses and the threatening letter they'd received just last week warning them to get off the land—she was at the end of her emotional rope and clinging for dear life.

Doc Willard, the town veterinarian, came out of Ulysses's stall, a grim look painted in the lines of his weathered old face. Nita felt tears prickling the corners of her eyes, but refused to let them flow over.

"I'm sorry, Nita. The break is too severe, and with his age…we're going to have to put him down."

"Ulysses was just an old workhorse, but he was Daddy's favorite. He's going to be crushed by this."

"How is your Pa?" Doc Willard asked. "I heard he took quite a spill when the horse went down."

"He's in surgery right now. The doctor's say he'll be off his feet for at least six weeks and he'll probably need physical therapy." Nita thought of her daddy, lying on the hard, dusty ground, his leg twisted and bloody after being launched from the horse's back. He'd been out checking the fence in the north corral when his horse stepped in a hole—one too large to be created by a prairie dog or a badger. None of their employees would be foolish enough to dig a hole there, so she knew it had to be another attempt to scare them away.

She also knew, no matter how vehemently they denied any wrongdoing, the Devlins were responsible for this. And this time they'd gone too far. Her daddy could have been killed.

A fresh round of tears burned their way up into her throat and she swallowed them back. She'd lost her mother to cancer when she was little, and later lost her older sister Rose to the lure of the big city. Nita didn't know what she would do if she lost her daddy, too. She would kill any man who tried to hurt him. But this situation was growing too big, too out of hand for even her to deal with.

She'd heard the Texas Cattleman's Club was a cover for some sort of mercenary group that traveled the globe dispensing justice and fighting for the greater good. She'd asked them for help a couple times already. They'd even sent a man over to look around, her best friend Alison's new husband Mark. He hadn't found anything that made him believe the Devlins were responsible, but Nita trusted that family about as far as she could spit. For more than one hundred years they had been trying to get their hands on the Windcroft land—the land they hadn't already stolen that is.

But like everyone else, including the police, the Cattleman's Club didn't want to get involved in the Windcroft-Devlin feud.

Maybe now they would, since people were getting hurt.

"You should be at the hospital," Doc said.

"Before he went into surgery, Daddy made me promise to come home and see to the horse. You know how he is, the farm always comes first." It was a quality he'd drilled into Nita from the day she was old enough to walk. She couldn't remember a time when she hadn't worked the horse farm at his side. And now that he was incapacitated, it was up to her to see that things ran smoothly.

Outside the stable she heard hoofbeats. "Do what you have to do with Ulysses, Doc," she said on her way out the main door. Outside, Jimmy Bradley, the stable manager, was dismounting his horse. The setting sun cast long, ghostly shadows, and the cool, dry air had her shivering under her heavy flannel shirt.

"Well," Nita asked. "What did you find?"

Jimmy took off his hat and wiped the sweat from his brow. "More holes, all through the north and south corral. We'll check the east and west corrals and the stallion pens tomorrow when we have more light. The boys will work through the night filling what holes we've found so far. Until it's safe we should keep the horses in the stables."

"You're sure it wasn't an animal?"

"No, ma'am, unless this particular animal digs with a shovel and leaves boot prints in the dirt. If I had to venture a guess, I'd say it's them damned Devlins."

Having been with the farm since before Nita was born, Jimmy was no stranger to the Windcroft-Devlin feud. "I can't disagree with you."

"Something needs to be done, ma'am."

Frustration tied her insides in knots. She'd never felt so useless. "I know that Jimmy, but without proof the police won't get involved. When I called them this afternoon, they said it was probably just some kids pulling a prank."

"This was no prank."

With the police unwilling to help, she knew she had only one choice left. Even if that meant swallowing her pride, dropping to her knees and begging. The safety of her family and her animals was worth the sacrifice.

She pulled her keys from her pocket and headed for her truck. "I think it's time I paid another visit to the Cattleman's Club."

Jimmy scoffed. "They wouldn't believe you before. What makes you think they'll listen now?"

She climbed into the truck and gunned the engine. "This time, I'll *make* them listen."

Connor Thorne stepped from the cool Texas night into the Cattleman's Club lobby, the scent of leather and cigars washing him over him and settling his soul. The club's paneled walls displayed oil paintings of members past and present, of whose ranks Connor had only recently joined. So recently, in fact, that he still felt a bit awkward breezing into the building unannounced.

But not for long. He was about to receive his first official assignment.

Considering the late hour the lobby was deserted. He'd come straight from the airport when he got the message from his brother saying an emergency meeting had been called. Connor had been in Virginia tying up loose ends after a very abrupt leave from the army. Of course the men from his platoon had insisted on throwing him an official going-away party. One that had lasted pretty much up until he boarded a plane that afternoon. He was functioning on about two hours of sleep and the remnants of a hangover.

Despite that, when he opened the door to the meeting room, he was filled with an uncharacteristic excitement, a sense of worth he'd not experienced since leaving the Rangers.

His identical twin, Jake, lounged in one of the maroon leather armchairs. Two of the other club members, Logan Voss, a successful cattle rancher, and Gavin O'Neal, the new town sheriff, stood around a table studying a copy of the map recently stolen from the Royal Museum.

"Connor, you made it." His brother rose from his seat and grasped his hand. "Thanks for coming in so late. We have a bit of an emergency on our hands."

"Not a problem," Connor said.

The other men turned to greet him, each shaking his hand, then they all took seats.

"I know you just got off a plane," Jake said. "You want a drink, something to eat?"

Connor knew his brother was only trying to make him feel welcome, but the gesture made him feel even more the outsider. "Let's get down to business."

"That's my brother," Jake told the other men with a good-natured laugh. "All work and no play."

Though Jake's words annoyed Connor, he couldn't deny the accusation. He always had been the responsible, serious twin. The worker. Jake had been the outgoing, charming one. The one to have all the fun and to get all the pretty girls.

Although, as a recently—and very happily—married man, Jake's-girl chasing days were definitely over.

"We got another visit from Nita Windcroft tonight," Gavin told him. "Looks like the Windcroft-Devlin feud is heating up. Or someone wants it to look that way."

"She barged right into the club again, demanding to be heard," Jake said, looking more amused than annoyed. "You've gotta admire her determination."

"I thought we weren't going to get involved in that," Connor said.

Jake filled him in on Nita's visit and the recent disturbances at the farm. "We might have believed she was trying to frame the Devlins but according to Alison, Mark's wife, Nita would never do anything to hurt her family. We think someone really is trying to scare them off the land, and we're not sure how far they'll go. We feel it would be wise to send a man out to the farm to keep an eye on things until we find out who's behind this. Considering your experience with the Rangers, we think you're the man for job."

Connor dashed a kernel of disappointment. It wasn't the international intrigue he'd been hoping for, the kind he'd grown accustomed to serving in the Special Forces. But no matter what the job, he would give it one hundred percent.

When given an order, he followed it to the letter.

"And Jonathan's murder?" he asked. "Are we still looking at Nita for that?"

"Alison swears she isn't capable," Logan told him. "We want to know what you think. Nita has agreed to let us move a man into the house. While you're there you can do some snooping around, see if there's any evidence we're over looking."

"Can you get away from the engineering firm?" Jake asked.

"Not a problem." Another week sitting behind a desk and he'd go psychotic with boredom.

He never would have considered a desk job, but his father had wanted to retire and there had been no one else to carry on the family business. As always, being the responsible one, Connor had set aside his own dreams to accept the duty.

The sad truth was, it had been so long since he'd followed his own heart, the path he'd once dreamed of walking had become so overgrown with other people's expectations, he would need a machete to chop his way through. Joining the Cattleman's Club was the first thing Connor had done for himself in a very long time. Maybe ever.

Despite that, Jake somehow always managed to outshine him. If he didn't love his brother so much, Connor may have resented him. But Jake was so charming, so full of playful mischief, it was hard not to get caught up in his energy. And he appeared to have outgrown his reckless tendencies. For the most part, anyway. Connor supposed marriage could do that to a man. Not that he would ever find out. Marriage and family weren't in the cards for him.

"What do you know about Nita Windcroft?" Logan asked.

"Not much." Connor had never actually met Nita, but he'd heard plenty of talk from the people in Royal. He knew she was raised by a single father and worked the farm by his side—an honest to goodness tomboy. Connor also had heard gossip that, if she didn't pretty herself up and find a man soon, she was fast on her way to becoming an old maid.

He had met his share of tough women in the military, the kind you wouldn't want to meet in a dark alley, and it sounded as if Nita Windcroft fit the bill.

"I know that if you have a horse that needs breaking, even the wildest, meanest of stallions, Nita Windcroft is the woman to call," Connor said.

The other men exchanged a look, and Connor got the idea there was something more to this than they were telling him.

"She's a pistol," Gavin agreed. "With pride by the bushel load."

"Why do I sense there's a problem?" Connor asked.

"She asked for a man to watch the *farm*," Jake clarified. "We think that with her father out of commission, she may be the next target."

"We believe she's in danger," Logan added. "We don't want you to watch the farm. We want you to watch *her*."

Now it was starting to make sense. "In other words, Ms Windcroft isn't going to be too keen on having a bodyguard?"

Jake nodded, a screwy grin on his face. "I'd say that's a fair assessment."

"So, you're okay with that?" Gavin asked. "Living in such close quarters with a woman like Nita."

Connor shrugged. "Sure, why wouldn't I be?"

They exchanged another look. This Nita person must be even worse than he'd imagined, in looks or personality—or both—if they thought he would be so put off by her that he wouldn't take the assignment.

"Who knows," Jake said, leaning over and slugging Connor in the shoulder, wiggling his eyebrows suggestively. "You might even like her."

Granted, Connor didn't date much, but he was far from desperate. And he preferred his women to look like…well, *women*. Round and soft in all the right places and reasonably attractive.

"I don't think we have to worry about that," he told his brother. "I'm definitely the man for the job."

"Then pack your bags," Gavin said. "She's expecting you first thing tomorrow morning."

Nine o'clock the following morning, gravel and dirt crunching under the tires, Connor drove his Mercedes up the long drive leading to the Windcroft horse farm. The sprawling, stone house looked fairly new considering how long the farm had been in the Windcroft family. The facade was punctuated with a lot of tall, easily accessible windows—a prowler's dream. He hoped they had a good alarm system, and if they didn't, they needed one.

Wood rocking chairs flanked the long, covered porch, and off to one side of the front yard a cedar swing sat amidst a pristine, green lawn in the shade of a towering oak whose leaves had just begun to turn yellow. In the distance, on acres of flat land, he could see barns and outbuildings, corrals dotted with mesquite trees. There was also another smaller, older house several hundred yards back from the main structure. He didn't know much about horse farms, and even less about horses, but this one seemed pretty damn big. Which explained why Nita Windcroft was so charged to get to the bottom of the threats and mischief. The sheer size alone meant he would have his work cut out for him.

The one thing he didn't see, however, was horses, which struck him as odd.

He parked, grabbed his things from the back seat and stepped out into the cool, dusty air. Duffel bag in hand, he climbed the stairs to the porch and knocked on the front door. Several minutes passed with no answer so he knocked again.

"Can I help you?" a feminine voice inquired and Connor turned to find a woman climbing the steps behind him. She was tall and slim, dressed from head to toe in work-faded denim and a pair of battered cowboy boots. A farm hand, he assumed. A fine-looking one at that.

And young. She didn't look a day past eighteen.

"Ma'am," he said, removing his hat. "Name's Connor Thorne."

Hands on her hips, she eyed him up and down from under the brim of a black Stetson, as if she wasn't quite sure what to make of him. Finally she said, "You're older than I thought."

"Beg your pardon?"

"You look older than your brother. But being twins, I guess you're not."

"You know my brother?"

"Of course I do."

He should have figured. Before Jake had settled down, he'd been a shark with the ladies, though this one looked a bit young even for him.

She removed her hat and a mane of shiny black hair spilled down around her shoulders. She gazed up at him with a pair of wide, startlingly brilliant violet eyes.

Holy cow, he didn't even know eyes came in that color. Whoever this girl was, she was a looker. At thirty-eight, he didn't typically date women young enough to be his daughter, but this girl had a fresh, wholesome quality that intrigued him.

He also had a job to do, one that would leave no time for a roll in the hay with a stable girl.

"I'm looking for Nita Windcroft," he said. "She's expecting me."

"Well—" she looked him up one side and down the other "—this is your lucky day, cowboy, because you just found her."

Two

Salvation manifested itself in many forms.

This particular brand had showed up in tight jeans, a flannel shirt and cowboy boots.

And he was looking at her as though her hair had caught fire.

"*You're* Nita Windcroft?"

"That's what it says on my birth certificate."

He shook his head, as if he couldn't believe it. Connor may have been Jake's identical twin, but they were complete opposites. Sure, they looked alike—the same height, the same dark brown hair, though Connor's was cut military short. They both had eyes the color of the Texas sky at dusk on a cloudless day—deep, relentless blue. But Connor seemed darker somehow, more intense.

The lines bracketing his eyes were carved deeper in

his skin, the worry lines in his forehead more pronounced. This man had obviously done his fair share of frowning. In their depths his eyes held the life experience of a man twice his age.

The things that man must have seen to have eyes like that.

"You're really Nita?" he asked, looking down one side of the porch, then the other, as if he expected the real Nita suddenly to appear.

"Not what you were expecting, huh?"

His eyes roamed over her, slowly. Deliberately. Something about the way he looked at her, the way he studied her features, made her feel self-conscious and exposed.

"Not exactly."

More like, *hell no*, considering the look on his face.

"I thought you would be…older," he said.

"If you got your information from the old biddies in town, you probably thought I was some nasty hag."

She could tell by the look of guilt in his eyes, that's exactly what he'd thought, but he was apparently too polite to tell her so.

"If you'd like, I could show you my driver's license."

He finally cracked a smile—even though it was just a little one—and the change in his face, the softening of his features knocked her for a loop. "No, ma'am, that won't be necessary."

"You can call me Nita," she said, extending a hand for him to shake.

He gripped it firmly. Not the sissy shake some men used on a woman, as if the slightest pressure would snap her like a dry twig. On the other side of that coin were the men who felt they had something to prove, the ones who turned the shake into some kind of contest of brute strength. Connor's handshake was just right.

Having him stay here, getting in her way, might not be so bad after all.

"I guess we should get this show on the road," Nita said. "I had Jane, our housekeeper, make up the bedroom in the guesthouse so you'll have some privacy."

He paused. "I'd prefer to stay in the main house if that's not a problem."

The only empty bedroom in the main house was right next to hers. The thought of this man sleeping within shouting distance gave her an unexpected little shiver of excitement. She wondered what he looked like when he slept. Did he lie on his stomach, his back? Did he wear pajamas or did he sleep in his birthday suit?

Maybe one day she'd be lucky enough to find out.

Or maybe she'd be better off not letting her imagination run off with her again. Her daddy always accused her of being too curious, too brazen, for her own good.

"You can stay wherever you'd like," she told Connor. "We've got plenty of room. I'm just grateful you're here to keep an eye on things. The staff have been instructed to assist you in any way possible."

"I appreciate that," he said—so somber, so serious and businesslike. He really was different from his brother.

"Well, okay, let's get you settled in." She reached for the door handle, but in a flash he'd grabbed it and opened the door for her.

Well, damn. She couldn't remember the last time anyone but her daddy had opened a door for her. To the farm hands, she was just one of the men, and was treated accordingly. That was the way she liked it. She had no delusions about the kind of woman she'd become. She wasn't pretty or worldly like her sister Rose, and she certainly wasn't what you would call feminine. She could drink any of the farm hands under the bar and was known to cuss a blue streak when the circumstances demanded it. She couldn't cook, and had no inclination to learn, and would rather muck a stall than clean a toilet. Not a dream wife by any stretch of the imagination.

Not any kind of wife at all.

Not that she didn't appreciate a good-looking man in a pair of tight jeans, she thought, taking a not-so-subtle peek at Connor's rear end as she eased past him into the house.

As Connor stepped in behind her, he gazed around the interior, at the cream-colored walls and French doors that opened to the office, up the wide staircase that led to the bedrooms. "Not your typical farmhouse."

"Nope. My momma was a city girl and my daddy knew she wasn't happy living in the old farmhouse, so he built her this one. I was just a baby when we moved in. Two years later cancer took her."

Most people would mumble some sort of apology, or words of regret. Connor only nodded.

Not the talkative type, was he?

"Kitchen's that way," she said, pointing to the right. "Meals are at 6:00 a.m., noon and 6:00 p.m. sharp. Jane's room is behind the kitchen. Through those doors over there is the office. The family room and Daddy's suite are at the back of the house."

"How is your father?" Connor asked.

"His surgery went well. He'll be home in a day or two, but he's going to be off his feet for at least a couple of weeks. It could have been a lot worse. If he hadn't had Jimmy, our stable manager, with him, who knows how long he would have laid there." She'd seen men hurt before, but when they cut away her daddy's bloody pant leg and she saw the bone jutting through the skin, she'd felt dizzy and sick to her stomach.

She'd never seen him looking so pale and weak and broken down. It disturbed her more than she would ever let on. He was her protector. Her hero. Larger than life and invincible. Even though she was a grown woman now, she wasn't ready to let go of that fantasy. Instead it had been snatched away. Stolen from her by the Devlins.

She turned to Connor. "We need to find out who did this."

There was fire in Nita's eyes, a volatile, vivid anger— one Connor recognized all too well—and he suddenly felt sorry for any man who dared cross her. But through the anger, he could see a flicker of something else, something that might have been fear or hurt. It was gone so quickly, he couldn't pin down the exact emotion.

"That's what I'm here for," he assured her. "We'll get to the bottom of this."

She gave him a brusque nod. "I'll show you to your room."

He hooked his bag over his shoulder and followed her up the stairs. Her boots echoed against the bare wood steps and her backside swayed temptingly in front of him. She may not have the overly accentuated curves and feminine sweetness some men liked, but something about her stirred a yearning in Connor, a deep longing he hadn't felt for a very long time. A recklessness that tempted him to throw common sense aside and act on his feelings.

As he always did in these cases, he shoved those feelings deep down and kept them under lock and key. He'd learned long ago not to let his emotions get away from him. When he did, bad things happened. People got hurt.

And pretty as she was, she could still be a murderer.

Nita led him down the hall to his room. "Jane will change your linens once a week and you'll find fresh towels in the bathroom closet," she said from the bedroom doorway. "There's only one bathroom upstairs so I hope you don't mind sharing."

"I don't mind." Connor set his bag on the hand-stitched quilt draped over the full-size bed. The room was decorated in creams and beiges with dark blue and green accents and the pine furniture looked to be antique. It was a small room, but he didn't need much space.

"If you leave your dirty clothes in the bathroom hamper Jane will wash them for you."

"I can do my own laundry."

Nita laughed—a husky, rich laugh. "You'll have to get through Jane first, and I'll warn you, she's temperamental as a rattlesnake when it comes to other people using her fancy new washer and dryer. Ever since I plugged up the drain and flooded the laundry room trying to do a load."

"Long as she doesn't mind," Connor said.

"Believe me, she doesn't. She takes a lot of pride in keeping the household running smoothly. Normally she would be here to greet you and show you around, but she's at the hospital with Daddy."

"She's been with you a long time?"

"Ever since Momma got sick. Jane practically raised me and my sister."

Which meant she would be unlikely as a suspect, but he had to consider every angle. Every possibility.

She nodded toward his bag. "Would you like some time to unpack and settle in?"

"No, ma'am, I can do that later. I'd like to get started. I'll need a tour of the house and the property."

"We'll have to be careful. The boys haven't gotten all the holes filled yet, and I don't want any more horses or people hurt. I'm assuming you can ride."

He hadn't ridden since he was a kid, but he was sure once he was in the saddle it would come back to him. "I'll manage."

"Well, then, why don't we head out to the stable?"

They started down the stairs, side by side, and Nita's scent drifted his way. She smelled like fresh air and dust and faintly of sweat. And something else, something sweet, and a little flowery. Since he couldn't imagine her wearing perfume, he decided it was probably her soap or shampoo. And it was distracting him.

Now he understood what his brother, Logan and Gavin had been alluding to when they asked Connor if he would mind working with a woman like Nita. They weren't worried that he wouldn't like her. They thought he might like her too much. But he wouldn't let this attraction he was feeling cloud his judgment.

"Tell me about this feud," he said to get his mind back on track. "I've heard a lot of rumors. What's it really all about?"

"It's been going on for over a hundred years. My

great-great-grandfather, Richard Windcroft, lost half his land to Nicholas Devlin in a poker game. The Windcrofts swore that he cheated, but the courts ruled in Devlin's favor. A few weeks later Nicholas was shot dead and my grandfather was blamed, but there wasn't enough evidence to convict him. We've been at odds ever since."

"Do you think Richard killed him?"

"He swore he didn't, and Windcrofts are honest men."

"So, if the Devlins are behind the threats, why do they want you off the land?"

"They've *always* wanted our land."

"But why now?"

Nita shrugged. "I don't know. Do they even need a reason?"

"Do you think there could be a connection to Jonathan Devlin's death?"

She stopped and spun to face him, her eyes dark with anger. "Don't think I don't know what people are saying. I may have hated Jonathan Devlin, but I didn't have anything to do with his death. Not me or anyone else here. You got that?"

Whoa. She didn't pull any punches. He hadn't known too many women who were so in-your-face direct.

"I don't listen to gossip," he told her. "Only facts. And right now, the facts don't point to the Devlins."

"If it's not the Devlins, then who would do this. And why?"

"That's what we're going to find out."

"It's the damndest thing," Jimmy Bradley said. He, Nita and Connor stood in the west corral studying one of the holes the farm hands hadn't yet filled. After touring the property, Connor understood how someone could dig holes in the more remote areas undetected. Under the cover of darkness, unless someone was out guarding the perimeter, it would be nearly impossible to see them. But whoever had done this one had dug not three hundred yards from the bunkhouse where the farm hands slept. The question was, why?

The holes were definitely made with a shovel, and the guilty party had left footprints in the fresh dirt. Connor crouched down and inspected the tracks. They were cowboy boots, and large, so he was guessing it was a man. Which could have been half the population of Texas for all he knew. Without a boot to compare it to, the prints wouldn't do him much good. He'd call Gavin and have a deputy come out and photograph them just in case.

One thing the prints did tell, him however, was that Nita hadn't done this—not that he'd thought she had.

"Could it be someone working on the farm?" Connor asked Jimmy.

"No, sir," Jimmy said with a firm shake of his head. "A few of the hands might be a little wild, but they're good, honest men and loyal to the Windcrofts. They would never do this."

Connor stood and brushed the dirt from his hands. "What about a past, disgruntled employee?"

"Well, there was one man we let go early last year," Jimmy said. "And it wasn't on the best of terms."

Nita shot him a deadly look. "He wouldn't do this."

"I need to know who he is and what happened," Connor told her. "I need to investigate every possible angle."

Her chin rose a notch. "His name is Sam Wilkins. The gist of it is, my daddy caught me and him in a...*compromising* position in the stable. Daddy asked Sam if he planned to marry me. When Sam said no, Daddy ran him off the farm with a shotgun."

Connor fought the grin that mental picture stirred up. "So, this man, he took advantage of you?"

The look she gave him was one of pure disdain, and her chin rose even higher. "Excuse me, but do I look like the kind of woman a man could take advantage of?"

At that very second, no. In fact, he was pretty sure she could hold her own with a grizzly bear. An emotion that felt like envy burned through him when he thought of the lucky individual who'd had his hands on that lean, lithe body of hers. He wondered if she'd be the shy, demure type in bed, or rowdy and assertive.

Something told him this woman didn't have a demure bone in her body. She would be full of passion and fire.

All the more reason to keep his thoughts on the assignment and off Nita. He wasn't looking to get involved with anyone—especially someone like her. The more attracted he was to a woman, the more desirable he found her, the more likely he was to lose control. And when he lost control, bad things happened. Which was the number one reason he hadn't been in a gratifying relationship with a woman in longer than he could remember.

"Besides," Nita said, drawing him back into the here and now, "last I heard he was foreman at his cousin's farm in Kentucky, so it couldn't have been him."

Connor was sure there was more to the story, but he had the suspicion he'd get his head bitten off if he asked. And she was right, it probably wasn't that employee. "Is there anyone besides the Devlins who has some kind of grudge against you?"

"I've asked myself that same question a million times and I just can't think of anyone."

"Maybe your father would know of someone?"

"I was planning to go visit him after we're finished. I can ask him then."

"If you don't mind, I'd like to come with you."

"Who's going to watch the farm?" she demanded.

He hadn't planned to come right out and tell her that he was assigned to be her bodyguard, and he had the feeling that when she figured it out for herself all hell would break loose. Either way, he was going to escort her to the hospital. If someone meant her harm he was going to be there to protect her.

"I'm sure Jimmy and the other men can keep an eye on things until I get back."

"We can do that," Jimmy said. The old man gave Connor a look, as if he had a pretty good idea that Connor wasn't there to watch just the farm.

"Besides," Connor said. "I doubt someone would be foolish enough to try something in broad daylight. Unless you think your father's not up to the company yet."

"If I know my daddy, he's already pitching a fit to get home. He wants to get to the bottom of this just as badly as I do. I'm sure he won't mind you coming."

"The sooner he gets back, the better," Jimmy said gruffly. "The boys went into town for supplies this morning and already there's been talk."

"What kind of talk?" Connor asked.

"That with Will gone, and all the disturbances out here, things are bound to fall apart."

Nita's face flushed with anger. "Don't those busy-bodies in town have anything better to talk about?"

"Why would they think that?" Connor asked.

"After word got around about the poisoned feed we lost customers," Jimmy said. "People pay top dollar to have their horses trained by Nita. If we can't guarantee a horse's safety, people stop callin'."

"All the more reason to catch the son of a bitch," Nita said, her eyes two violet embers.

Connor was convinced right then and there that Nita would never purposely cause trouble on the farm, not if it affected her livelihood.

"Seen enough?" she asked him.

He nodded and followed her out of the corral to where they'd left their horses. As they mounted, Nita noticed that he winced a little as he settled into the saddle. She often gave lessons to new riders and recognized the signs of a sore rear end. If he was achy from the short amount of time they'd been out, he'd be hurting like the devil by nightfall.

"We'll go this way," Nita said, leading him up the property line toward the main stable.

"How bad is it?" Connor asked.

"How bad is what?"

"Your financial situation."

She didn't want to discuss the farm finances with a stranger, whether he'd agreed to help her or not. It was no one else's business. And every time she let herself think about it, a new notch of fear worked itself into her side.

"We're holding our own," she told him. What she didn't say is that if business didn't pick up soon, if they continued to lose customers, it wouldn't be long before they went bankrupt. Then the Devlins would get what they'd been after all these years.

With her daddy out of commission, the burden of making things right landed squarely on her shoulders. But she could handle it. And when she found out who was trying to ruin them, that person was going to wish they were never born.

Three

When Nita and Connor stepped into her daddy's hospital room an hour later he was asleep, and Jane was perched in one of the visitor's chairs reading a romance novel—her one personal indulgence. 1:00 p.m. every afternoon, for exactly one hour she could be found on the cedar swing, or curled up on the couch, her nose buried in a book. Unless someone was bleeding to death or the house was in flames, everyone knew better than to weasel in on her "me" time.

Nita figured, under the circumstances, it would be safe to interrupt her. "Hi, Jane," she said softly.

Jane looked up, smiled and set the book down. Despite being away from the farm, she wore her typical work attire—plaid shirt, jeans and canvas tennis shoes—and her long dark hair was pulled back into a neat bun. She was nowhere close to the stunning beauty Nita's mother had been, but she had a quiet grace about her that Nita had always admired. And Jane didn't let anyone, especially the men on the farm, push her around. Though she was a good ten years younger than Nita's daddy, if anyone wore the pants in the Windcroft family, it was her.

"Hey, honey," Jane said, rising to give Nita a hug. Jane had been at the hospital late last night and had come back early that morning, and she looked tired for it. "How are things going at the house?"

"Breakfast was a bit of a fiasco," Nita said. "But I managed to get most of the burnt smell out of the house."

Jane cringed. "Lord, I don't even want to know."

Nita nodded toward the bed. "Has he been asleep long?"

"He's been in and out all morning. When he's not asleep he's complaining that he wants to go home."

"That sounds about normal." For as long as Nita could remember her daddy had hated hospitals, especially Royal Memorial. He'd never said so, but she figured it had a lot to do with her mother's illness. From what Nita had been told by her sister, who was old enough at the time to remember the chain of events, their momma had been feeling sick for a while but never went to the doctor. When she finally did, the cancer had spread so far there was nothing they could do but make her comfortable. She'd hung on for three months. Most of that time spent in this very hospital.

"Who's this young man?" Jane asked, giving Connor a curious look.

"Jane, this is Connor Thorne. He's going to be staying with us for a while, keeping an eye on things."

"Ma'am," Connor said, shaking her hand.

"Well, thank heaven for that," Jane said, glancing in Will's direction. "Things have gotten out of hand."

"Do you think it would be okay to wake him?" Nita asked. "Connor has some questions."

"Like a fella could sleep through all this chitchat," Will mumbled from the bed, gazing up at them through bleary eyes.

Nita moved to his side and took his hand, giving it a squeeze. He looked a hell of a sight better than he had yesterday. But propped up in the hospital bed, his leg in plaster from his foot all the way up to his thigh, he looked a decade older than his fifty-eight years—as if he'd aged overnight. "How are you feeling Daddy?"

"Like I keep telling the doctors, I feel fine. I'm ready to go home." He looked past her to Connor, who stood by the door, hands clasped behind his back, military straight. "You keepin' an eye on my girl?"

Connor gave a single nod. "Yes, sir."

Nita didn't correct her father by telling him Connor was there to watch the farm, not her. She'd let him believe that if it eased his mind.

"Daddy, Connor would like to ask you a couple of questions." She motioned for Connor to join her at his bedside. "He's trying to find out who did this."

"I know exactly who's responsible," Will said bitterly. "It was the Devlins."

"The truth is, there's just no evidence pointing to the Devlins and they've firmly denied any involvement,"

Connor told him. "Is there anyone else you could think of that has a grudge against you?"

He shook his head. "No one. It's the Devlins all right."

Connor could see where Nita got her stubborn streak. They looked alike, too. Same dark hair, same high cheekbones and proud chin.

"You just worry about getting better," Nita said, patting his hand. "I'll handle things."

Will smiled up at his daughter, pride shinning in his eyes. It amazed Connor how easy it was for some men to show the emotion. He'd strived for years to see that look in his own father's eyes. And despite all he'd done to please James Thorne, Connor still didn't feel he measured up. He probably never would.

"I want you to hire extra help," Nita's father told her. "Temporarily, until I'm back on my feet."

That chin of hers rose. "I can handle things just fine."

Connor had a feeling her resistance had little to do with her own abilities and everything to do with their financial situation. He suspected things were worse than she'd let on earlier that morning. And she probably didn't want to worry her father.

"Don't worry about things on the farm, Mr. Windcroft," Connor said. "I'll be helping Nita while I'm there."

He didn't know much about horse farms, but this gave him a good excuse to be close to Nita so he could keep an eye on her.

Nita flashed him an uneasy look, then turned to her father and smiled. "See, Daddy, I've got all the help I need. You just concentrate on healing."

Nita, Jane and her father chatted for a few more minutes, then Nita kissed him goodbye and she and Connor headed out to the parking lot. They'd barely cleared the door when Nita turned to him and said, "I didn't want to say anything in front of my daddy, but here's the thing. I really appreciate your offer to help out, but I can't afford pay you."

"I never asked you to."

Nita matched his long stride. "That's not the point. It wouldn't be fair for you to work for free."

"If I'm going to be there anyway, I may as well make myself useful." Connor pulled his keys from his pocket and as they neared the car, he unlocked the doors. "Besides, you are paying me. Room and board."

"What do you know about working a horse farm?" she asked.

"Not much." He opened her door for her, and though she hesitated and looked at him a little funny, she got in. He walked around and climbed behind the wheel, wincing as his backside hit the leather seat. Hell on earth, that smarted. How could a couple hours on a horse do so much damage?

"Do you know anything about horse training or breeding?" she asked.

He started the engine. "Nope, but I'm a fast learner."

"I don't know," she said, looking wary. "It just doesn't seem right."

"Nita, I'm not hurting for money, if that's what you're worried about. I'm set for life. Working for you isn't going to break me."

He could see her hackles rising. "So, what? Are you saying I'm a *charity* case?"

He shook his head. She did have pride by the bucket-load. "How about this? I'll help you out at the farm and you can teach me everything you know about raising horses."

"Like a trade?"

"Yeah, like a trade. Then it all comes out even."

She eyed him suspiciously. "You would want to learn?"

"Sure, why not? I like to learn new things."

"And while we're at it, I'll teach you to ride. Since you're looking a little—" she gave his backside a mean-ingful look "—*uncomfortable.*"

"It's that obvious, huh?"

"I'm just very observant," she said, and he could swear there was a suggestive lilt in her tone, in the way she let her eyes wander over him. She was the last woman in the world he would have expected to be a flirt, but here she was doing just that. And doing it well.

"So we've got a deal?" he asked.

She considered it a minute, then nodded. "Yeah, we've got a deal. Now, how about some lunch at the Royal Diner. With Jane gone there's no one to do the cooking and I'm starved. If I botch another meal the way I did breakfast, the men are gonna string me up by my toes. They said my cooking is about as appetizing as horse feed."

Connor let a grin slip through. He was feeling a bit hungry himself. "The Royal Diner it is."

Though some people preferred the fine French cuisine of Claire's, the Royal Diner would always be Nita's favorite. She loved the red vinyl booths and stools, the long counter where you could always find a friendly companion to share lunch with. She breathed in the scent of frying burgers and the mouthwatering tang of Manny's famous chili. But most of all, Nita liked it because her sister told her their momma liked to take them there. They would have burgers and milkshakes and their momma always gave them a penny for the gumball machine. Even though Nita didn't remember it, it was one more small connection, one link to the mother she wished she could remember.

"Can I take your order, folks?"

Nita looked up from her menu, expecting Sheila, the regular waitress. Instead she found Valerie Raines, the new, younger addition to the restaurant staff. She was a speck of a thing, skinny and petite, with eyes that made Nita think of shuttered windows. She was friendly enough, but always seemed a bit on the wary side, always on her guard.

"Hi, Valerie, I'll have a cheeseburger, fries and a soda."

"Sounds good," Connor said. "I'll have the same."

"And I'll take one of your sweet smiles," someone said, and all three of them turned to see Gavin O'Neal approaching the booth from the back of the diner. He flashed Valerie a charming grin. The Cattlemen Club men sure were a good-looking bunch, although Valerie looked less than impressed.

"Sheriff," she said, her eyes going from wary to ice-cold, before she turned on her heel and walked away.

"Whoa, talk about the cold shoulder," Connor said.

"What did you do?" Nita teased. "Leave her a lousy tip?"

Gavin shook his head. "I don't get it. I leave her a good tip and I'm sweet as candy to her but she seems inclined to dislike me. Must be the badge."

"Care to join us?" Connor asked.

"No, thanks. I was on my way out. I just wanted to stop and see how your father is doing."

"Better," Nita said. "He should be home in the next day or two."

"Glad to hear it. Give him my best," he said, and turned to Connor. "Your brother mentioned that you have experience reading maps. Is that true?"

"Some, sure."

"I'd like you to take a look at a copy of the map from the museum. I feel like we're missing something. Something obvious."

"I could come into the club sometime this week."

"I don't want to drag you away from your—" he glanced at Nita "—business. Why don't I bring it by Nita's place later this week, after Nita's father is feeling up to the company?"

"Nita?" Connor asked.

"Fine by me," she said. "I wouldn't mind getting a peek at that map to see what all the fuss is about."

"Settled then," Gavin said, dropping his hat on his head. "I'll see you two later this week. Enjoy your lunch."

When he was gone, Nita said, "Well now, aren't you Cattleman's Club men covert."

"What do you mean?"

"He doesn't want to drag you away from your *business?* Why doesn't he just say 'assignment'? That's what it is, right?"

"You asked for help, and I'm helping. That's all there is to it."

"Uh-huh. Whatever you say."

"Two cheeseburgers and fries and two sodas," Valerie said, unloading her tray onto the table. "Can I get you anything else?"

Nita shook her head. "Nothing for me."

"I'm good, too," Connor said.

Valerie reached in her uniform pocket for their bill, but as she pulled it out, it slipped from her fingers and fluttered to the floor. "Oops."

As she bent over to get it, a gold, heart-shaped pendant suspended from a delicate chain slipped from inside her uniform. Etched on its face were two intricately intertwined roses.

"Oh, my sister would love that," Nita said.

Valerie set the bill on the table and looked at Nita questioningly.

She pointed to the pendant. "Your necklace. Her name is Rose. She likes anything with roses on it."

"Oh!" Valerie pressed a hand over it and slipped it back beneath her collar.

"Did you get it here in Royal?" Nita was always on the lookout for a birthday or Christmas gift.

"Family heirloom." She flashed them a forced smile. "You two enjoy your lunch."

"She's an odd one," Nita said after Valerie was gone. "I'll bet she's hiding something. Some juicy secret."

"What makes you say that?"

"Everyone has a secret. Something they've done or said or felt that they don't want anyone to know."

"Oh yeah," Connor said, his interest piqued. "What's yours?"

Nita's violet eyes sparkled with mischief. "Well, if I told you, it wouldn't be a secret, now would it?"

Okay, so he hadn't really expected her to just blurt out that she'd done in Jonathan Devlin, especially after she'd so vehemently denied it that morning. But a tidy little confession would have been convenient. Though he had a tough time imagining her killing anyone, she did seem to have a quick temper. If she felt her family was threatened, who knows what she might be capable of?

They ate in silence for a while, and he could tell by the glances she kept shooting his way, the quiet would be short-lived. Finally she said, "So, tell me about yourself. Your brother says you used to be in the army."

"Rangers."

"Sounds exciting. Why'd you quit?"

Talk about secrets. When he'd left the military, it wasn't exactly by choice. "Just wasn't for me anymore," he told her—the oversimplified version of the events that led to his leaving.

"What do you do now?" she asked, then added with a knowing smile. "Besides your Cattleman's Club missions."

"My father retired recently and I took his place at his engineering firm."

"Engineering? Sounds boring."

"Someone has to do it," he said, even though she'd pretty much nailed it. Engineering bored him to tears. It always had, even in college, but he'd stuck it out and got his degree with the highest of honors, because it was expected. Thornes weren't quitters, his father liked to boast.

"But why you?" Nita asked. "Can't he sell the business?"

He sat back in his seat. "You sure do ask a lot of questions."

"Yeah, I have a curious nature. It gets me into trouble."

"You don't say." He didn't have any difficulty imagining that. She had trouble written all over her.

"Like the time when I was six and I played I'll-show-you-mine-if-you-show-me-yours with Bo Wilders behind the bunkhouse."

A grin tugged at the corner of his mouth. "Six, huh?"

"Don't tell me you never played that game."

"Not to my recollection."

"Well, Bo was bragging that he could pee on a tree, and made fun of me because I couldn't. Of course I had to prove him wrong, and you can imagine the mess that created."

Connor broke into a grin. "I can imagine."

"My daddy caught us and I got the whole birds-and-bees speech."

If Connor had been caught doing that, it would have cost him a lashing from his father's belt and a long lecture on respect and responsibility. As far as Connor could tell, his father had two expressions when it came to his sons—disinterest, and disappointment.

And maybe in Jake's case, exasperation.

"Sounds like you had an exciting childhood," Connor said.

"Yeah, that's one way to look at it. I'm not sure my daddy would agree with you, though." She polished off the last of her burger and took a long pull on her soda straw. "You about ready to go? We've got work to do."

Connor nodded. He pulled out his wallet and tossed a tip down on the table. "Let's get to it."

"I hope you know what you're getting yourself into," Nita said as they stood to leave.

"Don't worry about me. I can take whatever you can dish out."

"That's good," she said with a grin that could only be described as devious. "Because by the time I'm finished with you, you're going to be a full-fledged cowboy."

Four

Connor limped up the stairs to his bedroom. He'd always considered himself in supreme physical condition—until Nita got her hands on him, that is. He never imagined learning the proper way to ride a horse could do so much damage to a man's...*pride*. He ached something fierce in places he'd never ached before, in muscles he hadn't known existed until today. Rangers training had been a breeze compared to what she'd put him through.

After she felt confident he knew how to ride, and despite Jimmy's assurance that the boys had done a thorough job, she and Connor had gone out to make sure all the holes had been adequately filled and it was safe to let the horses back out to pasture. It was nearly dark before they rode back.

Since Jane wasn't there to cook, Jimmy had made a roaring bonfire and they roasted hot dogs on sticks. Afterward, they sat around the fire under a sky blanketed with stars drinking beer and swapping stories. Socially, the hands treated Nita like one of the men. An equal. But when it came to her running the farm, it was obvious they respected her authority and had no trouble taking orders from her. She was tough, but fair.

It had been a long day and now all Connor wanted to do was collapse in bed and sleep off the pain. Instead of going home and sleeping last night after receiving his assignment, he'd spent half the night doing his laundry and preparing for another who-knows-how-many days away from home. He'd had a total of about six hours sleep in the past three days. Hopefully, after a solid eight hours, he'd feel half-human by morning.

"You're walking a little stiff, there, Connor."

He reached the top landing and turned to see Nita climbing the stairs behind him, a self-satisfied grin on her face. She knew damn well what she'd done to him and looked awfully proud of herself for it.

"I've felt worse," he said. As a Ranger he'd been shot three times, nearly blown up and just about flattened like a pancake when his parachute opened late. Although the pain he was feeling tonight definitely ran a close second.

"The boys giving you trouble?" she asked.

"Boys?"

Her eyes traveled down to the vicinity of his crotch. "The family jewels."

He just about laughed out loud. He couldn't recall a ~man ever coming right and asking him about his *boys*. "The boys are fine," he assured her. "It's the rest of me that aches."

She followed him to his room. "There's a bottle of pain reliever in the bathroom cabinet."

"I think I just need sleep," he said unbuttoning his shirt. He grabbed his bag from the bed and tossed it on the floor. Unpacking would have to wait until morning.

"Tough guy, huh?" She leaned in the doorway watching him. "I think I know what might make you feel better."

"Oh yeah?" he asked. "What?"

She stepped in his room, lacing her fingers and cracking her knuckles. "Take off your shirt."

He looked at her, eyebrow raised.

She noticed the expression on his face and laughed. "Don't get your boxers in a twist. I'm only going to give you a back rub."

"A back rub?" Connor wasn't sure how he felt about that. Not that he couldn't use a backrub right about now, but they hardly knew each other. It might be…awkward.

"What's the matter?" she asked, walking toward him and rolling her sleeves. "Are you shy?"

He couldn't help wondering, by her taunting tone, if that was some sort of challenge. There was something about her, something wild and sexy and a little out of control. At the same time he'd never met a woman who seemed so confidant, so sure of what she wanted. It both intrigued and disturbed him. Intrigued him because, well, hell, who wouldn't be with a woman like Nita? She was a walking contradiction. A puzzle he was itching to solve. And that was exactly the thing that disturbed him. She had a way of making him *feel*.

Things he never let himself feel. Things he *shouldn't* feel.

"It's that curious nature of yours that I'm worried about," he told her.

"If I was making a pass at you, believe me, you would know it. I don't mince words."

"So I've noticed."

She propped her hands on her hips. "Well, do you want a back rub or not? I guarantee you'll enjoy it."

Oh, he didn't doubt that for a second. He just didn't feel it was proper considering they'd only met that morning. But the thought of not letting her made him feel like a prude.

"Yeah, what the heck," he agreed.

"Then take the shirt off and lay down on your stomach."

He shrugged out of his shirt and tossed it over the footboard, sat down and pried off his boots, then stretched out on the bed, laying his head on the pillow.

He felt the bed shift as Nita climbed on. She straddled his legs, plopped down and made herself comfy on the back of his thighs. Then her hands were on his shoulders, her skin warm and a little rough, her thumbs working themselves deep into the muscle. If he hadn't been so achy and exhausted, he might have been turned on by her touch, but the truth was, there was nothing sexual about her actions. All he felt now was relaxed.

Nita gave a low whistle, as her hands slid lower. "You military men sure do know how to grow the muscles."

If he wasn't half-asleep already, he would have ughed. "Out of curiosity, do you ever have a thought ou don't say out loud?"

"Cowboy, if you knew what I was *really* thinking, you wouldn't have let me anywhere near your bed."

He glanced over his shoulder and gave her a wary look.

She grinned. "I'm just pullin' your leg."

He settled his head down on the pillow and closed his eyes.

"And the answer to your question is no. I pretty much say whatever's on my mind. A lot of people don't appreciate that. They say it's not ladylike."

"Does that bother you?"

"Not really. I was born this way. If people don't like it, tough. I'm not out to impress anyone." She smoothed her hands over his skin. "What are all these marks on your back from?"

"Burn scars. I was a little too close to a building when it exploded."

"No kidding. And what about this one on your shoulder?" she asked, skimming her fingertips over it.

"Bullet wound."

"It looks recent."

"It was."

"Some covert mission you can't talk about, I'm assuming."

"Yep." He was fighting to stay awake, but he could feel himself beginning to fade, feel sleep overwhelming him. What the woman could do with her hands. He felt as if he were melting into the mattress.

She worked her hands lower, where he was the most sore.

"Hmm, feels good," he mumbled. So relaxed.

Nita dug her thumbs into the knots in his lower back. She was sure his backside was aching pretty good, too, and wondered what his reaction would be if she touched him there. She sure wouldn't mind. He had a body that wouldn't quit—wide shoulders and arms the size of tree trunks. A thick, muscular chest that tapered down into a firm torso and slim hips. And she could just imagine the equipment he was packing under those jeans.

Even though he was now technically her employee, she wasn't immune to all that strapping muscle and tanned skin. Not that a man being her employee had ever stopped her before. In fact, that made it all the more exciting. The stolen moments in the stable when no one was around. A quick roll in the field at sunset. Nights on a blanket under the stars after everyone else had gone to bed.

A little shiver of excitement passed through her when she thought of taking a tumble with Connor.

Those relationships—if you could even call them relationships—were always brief and uncomplicated. That was all men seemed to want from her, which worked out just fine since she'd never wanted to get married. She didn't even want to settle down. Not that she wouldn't enjoy the companionship. She might have thought about kids someday *way* in the future, someone to take over the farm someday. But in her mind, to have kids you ought to be married, and marriage meant compromise, losing your identity. She wasn't going to do that for anyone. Not after knowing what it had done to her momma.

Katherine had been from a wealthy Dallas family— a city girl. But when she'd met Will Windcroft she'd fallen desperately in love with him. She'd married him after only three months of courting and left the excitement of the big city for a simpler life on the horse-breeding farm. According to what Nita had been told, as happy as they appeared on the outside, deep down her momma missed her life in Dallas and never quite adjusted to the harsh conditions of the farm. But she knew Rose and Nita were happy there, and she loved Will too much to leave him. Not one to cause a fuss, she'd never told her husband how she felt, and tried to keep up the facade of the happy wife.

Nita sometimes wondered if the cancer had only been a symptom, and what her momma really died of was a broken heart. She would probably never know. What information she did have came from her sister and her mother's old friends. Her daddy, all these years later, still wouldn't talk about it. She knew there wasn't a day that passed that he didn't think about his wife and miss her terribly. Sometimes Nita would pass by his room and hear him talking to the picture of Katherine that he kept next to his bed.

She was sure Katherine was the reason why her daddy had raised Rose and Nita to be independent, to stand up for what they wanted and believed in. He taught them to follow their dreams and not compromise themselves for anyone or anything. Katherine was the reason why he hadn't made a fuss about Rose moving to the city instead of staying to help on the farm. Rose always had been like their mother in that way.

Nita heard a soft snoring sound and realized Connor had fallen asleep.

She sat back on his thighs and grinned. She really had worn him out. He'd done pretty well today considering his lack of experience. She had a feeling he was the adaptable sort, though she hadn't completely figured him out yet. He was so guarded, so...*controlled*. He seemed to say exactly the right thing all the time, whether it was what he was feeling or not. The concept was foreign to her, since, as they had determined earlier, she wasn't shy about speaking her mind.

She grazed her fingers over the puckered skin on his back. Burns, bullet holes—what he must have seen, must have been through. No wonder his eyes looked so old. So...wounded.

She very gently climbed off the bed and tiptoed to the door. She wouldn't mind getting into Connor's head, seeing exactly what made him tick. She wouldn't mind getting to know other parts of him as well. She wondered if a guy like him would be interested in a woman like her. It might have been her imagination, but when she'd stepped up on the porch that morning, before he realized who she was, she could swear she'd seen male appreciation in his eyes.

That, she decided, flicking off the light and glancing back at his peacefully sleeping form, would be something worth looking into.

"The number one rule on the farm is safety," Nita told Connor. She stood in the corral with Buttercup, a chocolate-brown mare.

Apparently her back massage had done the trick last night. He'd awoken that morning feeling refreshed and full of energy. So far he'd followed her through her daily routine and had learned how to feed and water the horses, how to muck a stall and how to put on a halter and saddle.

A great deal of what they did was hot, dirty, physically demanding work. But it was good, honest work. And though he couldn't put his finger on the exact reason, there was something about it that made him feel so...*peaceful.*

His orders now were to sit on the fence and observe as she trained the horse, and so he had for the past hour. Normally that would have had him crawling out of his skin, the way sitting behind a desk had. This was different. It was a beautiful fall day, with blue skies as far as the eye could see, and though the air was cool, the sun felt warm on his back and shoulders.

Simply watching Nita was a treat in itself. She had a way with the big graceful animals, some kind of second sense. She could anticipate the horses every move, every thought. It was obvious she really loved what she did, loved *them,* and the feeling was most definitely mutual.

It was all he needed to see to convince him there was no way she would ever do anything to hurt her animals. The poisoned feed, the holes—there was no way she could have done it herself. She just wasn't capable.

"When you approach a horse, especially in the corral, you never do it from behind," Nita said. "Horses have a blind spot and they get startled easily. Make sure she can see you. And approach from the left if you can."

"Why the left?" he asked.

"Because that's the side they're used to being handled on. Although Buttercup here is a big cream puff. It would take an awful lot to spook her. Isn't that right girl," Nita crooned, stroking the mare's neck. As if answering her, the mare lowered her big head and nudged Nita's shoulder.

"It's all about respect," she told him. "If you respect them, they'll respect you."

"You make it look so easy."

"Believe me, it's not always like this. I may not have bullet holes in me, but I've been bitten, kicked, thrown from the saddle and stomped on more times than I can count. I like the challenge." She stroked the horse's neck, affection in her eyes. "Not that I don't appreciate a horse like Buttercup every now and then."

"Is she yours?"

"She belongs to a family in Fort Worth. I'm training her for their daughter. I'll miss her, though. She's a real sweetheart."

"How long do you usually have a horse you're training?"

"It could take a month, sometimes two. Sometimes even longer. It just depends on what they'll be using the horse for, and how it takes to the training." She looked over at him. "You sure this isn't boring you to tears?"

He was finding it all quite interesting. Horse farming had never been something he imagined himself enjoying. The truth was, he never much considered anything but his chosen course, first with the army, then taking his father's place at the engineering firm, though technically speaking, that hadn't been chosen by him. He followed in his father's footsteps because that's what had been expected of him. To make up where his rebellious twin brother lacked.

Not that his father ever noticed.

"I'm sure," he told Nita.

She shrugged. "Okay. I guess we're about done here." She called to one of the hands and instructed the young man to take Buttercup and set her out to pasture with the other horses, then she and Connor walked toward the stable together.

"We need to talk about security for the house and the stables," he said.

"What kind of security?"

"An alarm to start."

She frowned up at him. "You really think that's necessary?"

"I do. Clint Andover, another member of the Cattleman's Club, is a security expert. I'd like to have him out to evaluate the property and tell you exactly what you would need."

She took off her hat and drew a sleeve across her forehead. "An alarm sounds expensive."

"I'm not going to lie to you. It probably will be."

"Connor, I can't—"

"Don't worry Nita, we'll figure something out."

Up went the chin. "I'm not a charity case."

"I'm not suggesting you are. I was thinking maybe you could set up some sort of deferred payment plan."

Meaning, he could pay Clint and when Nita made payments to Clint, he would divert the money back to Connor. It was the only way they could make it work, because he knew she would never take money from him.

It wasn't as if he couldn't afford it. He lived a pretty simple life. Being in the Rangers meant active service, and missions all over the world at a moment's notice. He could be gone for weeks, sometimes months, at a time. The less complicated his life, the better. No house plants to water, no pets to board, no significant other left behind to wonder if he would return home in a pine box.

And he'd grown so used to living that way, it was permanently ingrained in his personality. He had more money than he would ever spend sitting around gaining interest. It seemed a waste not to use it on something.

"I don't like the idea of owing anyone money," Nita said.

"At least let me call him and see what he has to say. It's worth the safety of the people and the animals here. And it could be good for business."

She looked up at him, squinting against the afternoon sun. Even with her eyes half-closed they were the brightest he'd ever seen. "How do you figure?"

"If you can advertise that you have a state-of-the-art security system, that would eliminate the threat of having the horses harmed. You could very well get back the business you lost."

Nita shook her head, her mouth in a grim line.

"What's the matter?"

"This is so wrong. Five years ago, we would have never even considered needing an alarm to keep the animals safe. It's the Devlins doing this."

"You don't know that."

"Yes, I do."

Nothing he said, no argument he could make, would convince her otherwise. "At least try to keep an open mind until we get some proof."

"And when is that going to happen? It feels like all we're doing now is sitting around waiting for the next attack."

"People are working on it."

"The Cattleman's Club," she said, and he only looked at her.

"Should I make the call?"

She hesitated for a second, then shrugged "What the heck. I guess it can't hurt to hear what the man has to say."

He pulled out his cell phone and dialed. When Clint's secretary answered, she told him Clint would be out of town a couple of days, but would get back to Connor as soon as possible.

He relayed the message to Nita. "I'll let you know when he calls me."

They continued toward the stable when Nita heard a car engine, and turned to see a dark BMW pulling up the driveway.

"Who is that?" Connor asked, stepping slightly in front of her, something she was sure he did automatically, from being in the military.

"That would be Gretchen Halifax."

"Gretchen Halifax? What does she want?"

It was pretty obvious Connor didn't like the woman, not a big surprise considering she was running against his brother for mayor. "Probably to see her horse. We board him for her."

"That bitch-on-wheels has a horse? What for?"

"How should I know? It's business. She's one of the few boarders I have who didn't pull out after the feed was poisoned. I may not like her, either, but her money is as good as anyone else's."

Gretchen parked close to the house and got out of her car. She was dressed in a business suit and high-heeled pumps, and her hair was professionally sculpted into an indestructible shell. The woman reeked of old money. "Hello, Nita," she called.

"Hello, Gretchen." Nita walked over to meet her and noticed that Connor hung back, his Stetson pulled low. She took in Gretchen's designer outfit. "Guess you're not here to take Silver Dollar for a ride."

Gretchen smiled that phony, politician's smile of hers. The one that made Nita's skin crawl. "Not this time. I just happened to be in the area and I wanted to come by to tell you how sorry I am that your father was hurt. Is he going to be all right?"

"He'll be good as new in no time. Thanks for asking. Gretchen, have you met Mr. Thorne?"

Nita waved Connor over knowing that with his hat on Gretchen could easily mistake him for Jake, which, considering the fleeting look of distaste on her face, she had.

"Connor Thorne," Nita added. "Jake's brother."

"What a pleasure." The plastic smile slid into place and she held out a hand for him to shake.

With a slight hesitation, Connor shook it. "Ms. Halifax."

When Gretchen turned to Nita, Connor wiped his hand on his pant leg.

"I'm not one to listen to rumors," Gretchen said. "But I've heard you've fallen into hard times. Is there anything I can do to help?"

How about you throw on a pair of boots and muck a stall, Nita was tempted to say, but held her tongue. "We're okay, Gretchen, thanks for asking."

"I've always admired your family and their hard work. I'd even consider a partnership with you if it came down to it."

Over my dead body, Nita thought, wondering what

the woman could possibly gain by offering her help. Women like Gretchen Halifax didn't do anything out of the goodness of their hearts. She used people for her own personal gain. Maybe by owning a farm she thought she would be closer to the community somehow. No matter the reason, it would be a cold day in hell when Nita let Gretchen weasel her way into the family business.

"Those are just rumors," Nita assured her. "We're doing fine."

"I'm so glad to hear it. You take such good care of Silver Dollar."

And how she knew that, Nita wasn't sure. Gretchen rarely came to see the horse and had only ridden her once for a photo shoot. Nita figured she'd bought it as some sort of campaign ploy, part of her political image.

"She's a sweet horse," Nita said.

"When I'm mayor," Gretchen said, casting Connor a challenging look, "I'll pressure the sheriff to put an end to the Windcroft-Devlin feud. And with the new policies I'll be enforcing, you'll be eligible for tax breaks that will benefit your business."

Blah, blah, blah. Nita resisted rolling her eyes. If Gretchen thought that little pitch was going to win her Nita's vote, she was wasting her time. Nita didn't have anything against the woman personally. She just had a distaste for phony, self-serving people in general.

"Thanks for stopping by, Gretchen." As in, get lost.

"Remember, if there's anything I can do to help, don't hesitate to call." Gretchen picked her way across the gravel drive and got into her car, waving before she drove away.

"I feel like I need to go wash my hand," Connor said from behind Nita.

"Why?" Nita teased, turning to him. "She give you cooties?"

He had a look of thorough disgust on his face. "Does she really think people fall for that fake nice routine?"

"I hear that Malcolm Durmorr is smitten with her."

"Malcolm is even sleazier than she is," Connor said.

"What'd she want?" Jimmy called to them. He was loading tools into the back of the pickup.

"Came to see how we're doing," Nita told him, walking over to the truck. "Wants to help out if she can."

Jimmy shook his head. "That one gives me a serious case of the creeps."

"You off to fix those fences?"

He tossed a bundle of precut wood boards in the bed. "Yep. It should take most of the afternoon."

"I'll be in the office for the rest of the day," Nita said. "Why don't you take Connor with you?"

"Actually, I think I'll hang back," Connor said. He didn't like the idea of Nita in the house all by herself. On the off-chance that someone would risk harming her in the middle of the afternoon, he was going to be there to intervene.

"There's nothing for you to do in the house and Jimmy could use the help."

He could see this was going to be a problem, and looked to Jimmy for a little help. The old man picked up on his silent plea.

"It's nothing I can't handle on my own," Jimmy told Nita.

"I know it isn't, but it'll go a lot faster with another

man helping, and Connor wanted to learn all about raising horses. That means everything." She pinned her eyes on Connor. "Even the things you don't think are much fun."

"This is not about the entertainment value of the work. And I'm going to regretfully decline."

"Regretfully decline?" She propped her hands on her hips and her eyes turned stormy. "According to our arrangement, you work for me now. That means taking orders."

He held his ground, but he didn't see this ending well. She'd dug her heels in and it looked as if she wasn't going to budge. "I'm sorry, but I can't do that."

Her anger level went from zero to sixty in about half a second. "You're here to keep an eye on the farm, aren't you? So go keep an eye on it!"

He was going to have to tell her the truth about what his real orders were. And she wasn't going to like it. "I'm not here to protect the farm," he said.

Now she just looked confused. "Then what the heck are you here for?"

"I'm here to protect you."

Five

"The *hell* you say?"

"We think that with your father out of commission, you could be the next target. I've been sent here to make sure you remain safe," Connor explained.

"Well, I'm touched by your concern," she said, even though she wasn't, even though she wanted to tell him to take a hike. "But I can take care of myself. What I need is someone to watch the farm."

"I've been given orders and have every intention of following them."

"Oh, *now* you admit that you've been given orders? Well, here's an order for you pal, get out there and fix that fence or pack your bags." She turned and stomped toward the house, anger burning a hole in her gut. Who the hell did these Cattleman's Club guys think they were? She was perfectly capable of defending herself. She didn't need a keeper.

"You don't want to do that," Connor said, following her.

She flung the back door open and hurled herself through it. "And why is that?"

"Because when I go, the Cattleman's Club will pull out completely and you may never know who's behind the disturbances. This situation will continue to get worse until you lose everything. Do you want to be responsible for driving your family business into the ground?"

She spun around, found him standing in the doorway looking smug as hell. "Then I'll go to the police."

"Are you forgetting who the sheriff is?"

Another Cattleman's Club member. Swell. She was beginning to wonder if seeking their help had been such a hot idea after all. "What is this, a conspiracy?"

He walked toward her, his voice low and patient. "If you calm down for a minute, and think of this logically, you'll see that we're only trying to help. And it would be in your best interest to let us do that."

She took a long deep breath, felt the initial spark of anger begin to subside. Logically she understood their reasoning, and she did need their help. She may be hot-headed but she wasn't stupid. She just didn't like losing control, having her freedom determined by someone else. Her every move monitored.

She didn't seem to have a whole lot of choice, though.

"Let me keep you safe, Nita."

Something in the way he looked at her, the sincerity in his eyes, made her feel warm all over. It was almost as if he cared about her, and didn't just want to get into her pants. In fact, he didn't act that way at all.

"I'll go along with this," she finally said, then added for good measure, "But I'm not going to like it."

"Doesn't matter if you like it, as long as you're safe."

She supposed, if she had to be stuck with a man twenty-four/seven, she'd be hard-pressed to find a better-looking one. Not only that, but he was nice. A little on the reserved side maybe, but he definitely had potential. Being in such close quarters would give her a chance to pick that brain of his, to see what made him tick.

It also gave them time for some good old-fashioned horizontal fun.

Nita had just finished paying the monthly bills when she heard a car pull up the driveway. Jane was back with Will.

Nita stuffed the checkbook in the drawer and closed her laptop computer. When she opened the office door she found Connor right where she'd left him, sitting on the bench in the foyer, reading, of all things, one of Jane's romance novels.

"Good book?" she asked.

He gazed up at her with an aren't-you-funny look. "I was bored and it was all I could find."

"You should have asked. Daddy has a slew of books in his room. Espionage novels mostly."

"I'll remember that next time." He set the book down next to him. "Someone is here."

"I know. It's probably Daddy and Jane."

He unfolded himself from the bench and rose to his feet. "I should give them a hand."

Nita opened the front door and Connor followed her out. Jane was standing at the open truck, grabbing the bags, and Will was trying to boost himself from the front seat while negotiating a pair of crutches, his cast stuck out awkwardly in front of him.

"I'll help you, Daddy," Nita called to him and told Jane, "I'm so glad you're back. We missed you around here."

"Well," Jane said, shooting Will a lethal look, her voice tight. "It's good to know *someone* around here appreciates me."

"I'll get those bags," Connor told her.

Jane thrust them at him then stalked into the house. Whoa.

She definitely had a temper, but she also had a long fuse. It took an awful lot to get her that riled up.

"What's the matter with her?" Nita asked Will as she helped him to his feet.

"She's got herself in a dither over something," he said, leaning on his crutches. "As long as I live I'll never understand women."

"Let's get you settled in then I'll go talk to her."

She helped him inside, got him seated comfortably on the couch in front of the big-screen television, then brought him painkillers and a glass of water.

"Can I get you anything else?"

"I don't think so," he said, patting her arm. "It's just good to be home. I hate hospitals."

"I'm leaving."

Everyone turned to see Jane standing in the doorway, a suitcase in her hand. Her face was devoid of emotion, but Nita could see barely contained anger not so far under the surface and her voice was as high and tight as an overstretched guitar string.

"Leaving?" Nita asked. "Where are you going?"

"To stay with a friend in Odessa."

Boy, Jane really was mad if she had to leave for a few days to cool off. And the timing couldn't have been worse. Nita didn't have time to take care of the farm *and* her daddy. She hoped whatever was eating Jane, she would get it out of her system soon. "When will you be back?"

"I won't."

Nita was sure she'd heard her wrong. "Say again?"

"I said, I'm not coming back."

For a second, she too stunned to form words. "B-but…you *have* to come back."

"I left my forwarding address in the office. You can send my last check there."

She started to turn, and Nita shouted, "Wait a minute! You can't just leave. You're part of the family. You belong here with us." She turned to her daddy who sat stone-faced, his eyes on the television. "Daddy say something."

"Yes, Will," Jane said. "Say something."

His mouth clamped tighter into a hard, stubborn line.

Nita turned to Jane, a sick feeling rolling around in her belly when she saw the determined, stubborn look on Jane's face. Nita had seen that look enough times to know Jane meant business.

No. There had to be a way to fix this. Jane couldn't go. Being the only other female on the farm, she was Nita's only ally, her confidant. Jane understood Nita in a way no one else ever had, and never once judged her for her unconventional thinking. She wasn't just a housekeeper, she was *family*.

"Tell me what happened," Nita said to Jane, feeling desperate. "What can we do to fix this?"

"Why don't you ask that hardheaded old fool? I have to go." Jane spun on her heel and a minute later Nita heard the front door slam. She turned to her daddy.

"What happened? What did you do to her?"

"I don't want to talk about it."

"Nita, I'm going to go see if Jimmy needs me for anything," Connor said. He must have figured Will might be more willing to talk without an audience. Either that, or he didn't want to get involved. Not that she blamed him. It was her own family and she didn't want to have to deal with it. She just wanted everything to go back to normal.

"That's fine," she told Connor. "I'll be out there in a bit."

When he was gone, she turned back to her daddy. "Jane, a member of our family, just walked out that door and you damned well better want to talk about it."

"I'll hire a new housekeeper."

Jane was right about one thing, he was hardheaded. Nita sat on the edge of the couch. "Daddy, please talk to me. What happened?"

He mumbled something Nita didn't catch. "What was that?"

"I *said,* she told me she *loves* me."

Nita let out a surprised laugh. And here she'd thought something horrible had happened. "Is that all?"

He looked at like she was nuts. "What do you mean, *is that all?*"

"Are you telling me you didn't know? Jane has been in love with you as long as I can remember. Since you never dated I thought...well, I thought maybe you two had something going on the side."

He looked downright scandalized. "Of course not!"

"Do you have feelings for her?"

"She's been my friend for a long time."

"I'm talking about romantic feelings."

His dark eyebrows pulled into a frown. "That part of me died along with your mother."

How sad that would be if it were true, but Nita didn't believe it for a minute. He was an affectionate, caring person. She was sure he could love again if he'd only let himself.

"When Jane told you she loved you, what did you say to her?"

"I told her that in my heart I'm still married to your momma, and I made a vow to be faithful to her."

Nita winced. That one had to sting. To be rejected for the ghost of a marriage long since dissolved. "Daddy, Momma's been gone almost twenty years. She would want you to be happy."

"I *am* happy. I have you and Rose and I have the farm. I don't need a woman to complete me."

Nita sighed. There was no reasoning with him now. Poor Jane had to be devastated. To wait so long to speak her mind only to have her feelings shot down. No wonder she'd left. And Nita would miss her something fierce if she couldn't convince her to come back.

Jane had been around for so long Nita couldn't even imagine life without her. She'd cooked and cleaned and made sure the house ran like a greased wheel, had taken care of them all when they were sick. She'd been the female confidant Nita and her sister Rose had needed growing up. Jane had taken them shopping to buy their first bras, explained about periods and womanhood when the time came. But she'd never once overstepped her bounds and tried to take their mother's place.

She'd been like a wife to Will in every way besides the bedroom. They played hours of Gin Rummy, watched movies together and bought each other special gifts for Christmas and birthdays. And Nita suspected that deep down, though he wouldn't admit, he loved Jane, too.

After all these years, Nita didn't understand how he could let her go without a fight.

"I don't want to talk about this anymore," Will said. "What's done is done. Tomorrow you can go into town and pick up a paper. We'll look in the classifieds and find a new housekeeper."

"Whatever you say." Nita patted his arm. Let him think it was resolved. Little did he know, the discussion was far from over.

"I think I should come home for a while."

"Rose, there's nothing you can do here." Nita cradled the phone between her ear and shoulder while she removed a pan of charred potatoes from the stove and dumped it in the sink.

"With Daddy down and Jane gone things are bound to get crazy around there," her sister said. "I can help."

Nita ran cold water in the pan to stop it from smoking. Instead it sizzled and snapped and sprayed grease all over the sink and counter. Whoops.

She waved away the cloud of steam that billowed up in her face. "We're doing fine," she lied. "I can handle things."

Jane had only been gone three days and the entire

house had fallen apart. Dirty clothes overflowed from the laundry room, dishes from yesterday's breakfast were still stacked on the kitchen counter, and once again she'd annihilated dinner. One more night without a decent meal and the hands were going to up and quit on her.

"I'm worried about you. I'll feel better if I'm in Royal."

It wasn't that she didn't want to see Rose, and God knows she could use the help, but Nita knew her sister preferred the city. She would go stir-crazy being on the farm. Nita would never ask her to compromise her happiness by coming home.

"Rose, you don't have to do that."

Connor walked up behind her and looked over her shoulder into the sink, one eyebrow lifted. He'd just showered and put on fresh clothes and, boy, did he smell good. Like fabric softener and some kind of masculine soap.

"It's been ages since I've visited," her sister said. "I miss you guys."

"And you'll be here next month for Thanksgiving." Nita might have been imaging it, but she swore she heard sadness in her sister's voice and wondered if there was something wrong, something Rose wasn't telling her. Rose always had been the type to hold things inside, while Nita let the entire world know what was eating her. "Unless you need to come home now."

"Of course I don't *need* to. I just thought you could use the help."

"Nope, I've got things under control."

"Well, if you want me to come, don't hesitate to call."

They said their goodbyes and Nita hung up the phone.

"You've got things under control, huh?" Connor said.

She shot him a scathing look, even though she knew from the grin on his face, he was only teasing her. "Oh, be quiet."

"What was that?" he asked, nodding toward sink. "I smelled it all the way upstairs."

"Potatoes. I guess I had the heat in the pan too high. I was trying to cook them fast to catch up with the chicken."

"I don't think it works that way."

"I guess not. At least we'll have the chicken."

He looked around the kitchen. "Where is it?"

"I left it in the oven so it'll stay warm."

"I hope you turned the temperature down."

"Of course I did," she snapped. At least, she'd *meant* to. They simultaneously turned to look at the display on the stove.

"See," she said smugly. "It's on low. As in, not too hot."

Connor didn't look impressed by her stroke of genius. "I'm no gourmet, but on my stove the broiler settings are high and low and the regular oven is by temperature."

Her heart slid south into her belly. There was no way she could have ruined another entire meal.

She yanked open the oven door and smoke rolled out to join the cloud already hanging in the air from the potatoes. "Oh no!"

Connor grabbed an oven mitt, pulled the pan out and set it on the stove. The chicken was completely charred on one side and still smoking. "One side is okay...sort of. Maybe if you cut off the burned part?"

He had every right to be smug about it, but he wasn't, and, although she appreciated his encouragement, they both knew she couldn't serve chicken this burned to the men. They would accuse her of trying to poison them.

It wouldn't be the first time that week.

"Dump it," she said. She grabbed a newspaper from the kitchen counter and waved the smoke toward the open kitchen window. "I just wasn't meant to be in a kitchen. I think I was born without the cooking gene."

Connor dumped the chicken in the sink with the potatoes and set the pan back on the stove. "I have an idea."

"What idea?"

He pulled his cell phone out and dialed.

"Who are you calling?" Please let it be someone who knew how to cook.

"It's chili night at the Royal Diner."

Nita felt herself begin to salivate. Manny's chili was the best in Royal—hell, probably the entire state of Texas. But what about the men? They had to eat, too.

When Manny answered, Connor ordered chili with all the fixings. Enough to feed everyone, saving her from an inevitable mutiny. It wasn't the first time he'd saved her butt the past couple of days. She owed him big time, and could think of a couple of fun, mutually gratifying ways to pay him back.

They drove into town together to pick up the food, then after dinner he helped her clean the kitchen until it was spotless. He even did a couple of loads of laundry for her since he knew how and she was in no mood to mop up a flood.

Later, after Nita got her daddy settled in his suite and was on her way upstairs to get ready for bed, she realized she'd ruined dinner three nights in a row, fed him sandwiches for lunch and cold cereal for breakfast, yet

Connor hadn't uttered a word of complaint. He'd even insisted on paying for dinner tonight.

He hadn't made fun of her for not having a domestic bone in her body the way some men had. And he hadn't acted all high and mighty when he'd fixed things for her. He was so reserved, so guarded sometimes it was frustrating. But there was a fire burning in him, a passion he kept buried deep inside, she just knew it. She'd been so busy holding things together the past couple of days, and fell into bed so dead tired every night, she hadn't had time to even think about a seduction. Maybe, after a relaxing hot shower, it was time she paid Connor back for all his good deeds.

She might not have known how to operate an oven, but she sure knew what to do to set a man on fire.

Six

Connor checked all the windows and doors, and when he was sure the house was locked up tight, he trudged up the stairs to his room. The bathroom door was closed and he could hear water running. Nita was taking a shower. He fought to block out a sudden image of her naked and wet, but it slid through his brain and lodged itself there to torture him.

He walked into his room and closed the door, wishing he could leave the erotic image in the empty hall. Every time he was near Nita, he found himself wanting to touch her, wanting to taste that sassy mouth of hers.

Everything about her fascinated him. The way her silky raven hair shined when the sun hit it. How her violet eyes brightened or darkened depending on her mood. He never tired of watching her. The graceful flow of her body as she worked with a horse, the pure joy on her face that said she was doing exactly what she wanted to, what she was meant to do.

And if the sexual attraction wasn't bad enough, he really liked her. She was so feisty and full of life. The way she'd been looking at him with blatant interest the past couple of days both intrigued him and made him uneasy. He couldn't meet her eye, couldn't face the honesty there without his feelings getting away from him. If he allowed himself to let go, nothing good could come of it. Things would get out of hand and someone could get hurt. *She* could get hurt.

Still, he'd never met a woman who made him want to lose control the way Nita did.

He stripped off his shirt, tossing it over the footboard. He had just unfastened his pants when he was interrupted by a knock. He zipped back up and opened the door. Nita stood in the hall, her long hair wet, dressed in an oversize men's shirt that wasn't buttoned very high.

Aw hell.

When he should have closed them, his eyes wandered lower instead, and what little breath he had left backed up in his chest. If he'd ever wondered whether or not she had nice legs, he just got his answer. The shirt stopped at midthigh, and that exposed a lot of silky, milk-white bare skin.

"Can I come in?" she asked.

Though his head was saying no, his body didn't listen. As if in some sort of sexual trance, he backed up and held the door open wider.

She stepped inside and shut the door behind her,

leaning against it, as if she was making sure he couldn't get away. Her eyes fixed on him, wandered across his bare chest, then lower to his partially unfastened pants.

She was looking at him as though she'd been starved for a month and he was an all-you-can-eat buffet.

This was not good.

"I wanted to thank you for all your help this week," she said, "with Daddy and with the farm. I couldn't have done it without you."

He had a feeling he knew exactly how she wanted to thank him. He backed away a safe distance, keeping his face stony and disinterested. "No need to thank me. I'm sure you would have managed just fine without my help."

She stepped toward him, unfastening one of the buttons on her shirt, widening the V of smooth pale skin, so he could make out the curve of her breasts. "Maybe I *want* to thank you."

He held his ground, but he could feel his body reacting to her presence, to the scent of her freshly scrubbed skin. A warm curl of need started in his groin and spiraled outward. "As I said, that isn't necessary."

She propped her hands on her hips and gazed up at him. "Boy, you sure don't take a hint."

"I understand exactly what you're…suggesting. I'm declining your offer."

She popped another button on her shirt, till a lone button was all that kept him from pure heaven. "I'm not looking for a commitment if that's what you're worried about. Just some good clean fun. And if you want to play dirty, that's okay, too."

"And I'm still not interested," he lied. The truth was he wanted to rip off that shirt, and whatever she might be wearing underneath, and take her right up against the door. He wanted to feel those silky legs wrapped around his hips, feel her nimble body pressed up against him.

"I may look and act like a boy, but I'm still a woman, Connor." She undid the last button on her shirt, slowly eased it off her shoulders and let it slip to the floor. She wore plain white cotton panties—not what most men would consider overtly sexy. But combined with the woman underneath, they had fire pumping through his veins. Her skin was pale ivory and looked flawlessly smooth. Her breasts were small and pert, her nipples two tiny, dark points begging to be touched.

Longing swept through him in a hot rush, but he beat the feeling down. With most women he had no trouble keeping his emotions in check. He could see to his physical needs without letting his feelings override his good sense. Not that the encounters had ever been particularly satisfying. For him or his partner. But they had been safe, and that was all that had mattered. He knew with Nita he already was invested emotionally. Once he let go, let the sex happen, there would be no stopping him.

"Trust me, Nita, you look nothing like a boy. All the more reason for you to put your shirt back on."

She flashed him a teasing grin. "What's the matter, Connor, you don't like women? Is it that army, don't-ask-don't-tell thing?"

"Of course I like women." He knew she was only teasing—taunting—him and he yearned to take her in his arms and prove just which way the barn door was swinging. But he would lose control. He could hurt her.

"Are you always this...*forward* with men?" he asked,

though he had a pretty good idea the answer was a big fat yes.

"When I see something I like, I go after it. Is there anything wrong with that?"

"I guess that just depends on who you're after." He could see that she'd set her sights on him, but she had no idea what she was getting herself into. He was a ticking bomb, one she didn't want to be anywhere near when he finally detonated. "Whatever you think you know about me, you're wrong."

"I've seen the way you look at me." She spread a hand over her stomach, slid it slowly upward, across her rib cage and over her breast. She cupped it, pinching the nipple lightly, her lids heavy with desire, and Connor nearly groaned. "Your eyes don't lie. No matter how hard you try to hide it."

She stepped closer, until the tips of her breasts touched his bare chest. He sucked in a breath, felt his control slip another notch. For a woman who considered herself unfeminine, she sure did know how to seduce a man.

He clenched his hands into tight fists at his sides, so he wouldn't give into the urge to touch her. "You don't want a man like me, Nita."

"Why not?"

"I'm damaged goods."

She cupped a hand over the bulge in his jeans, rubbing him through the heavy denim. "Everything seems to be working fine."

He wanted to grab her hand, make her stop, but the second he touched her, it would be all over. And he couldn't look at her any longer without devouring her.

He closed his eyes. "I'm here to protect you."

Her breath was warm and sweet on his chin. "What has that got to do with us having sex?"

"I'm protecting you."

"From *what?*"

"From *me.*"

She stroked the skin just under the waist of his jeans and the muscles in his stomach spasmed. "Why the heck would I need protecting from you?"

"You wouldn't understand."

"I'm not afraid of you, Connor." She slipped her fingers lower, inside his boxers, and his legs went weak. "Let me make you feel good."

When she brushed against the tip of his erection, it was more than he could take. He grabbed hold of her arms and backed her against the nearest wall. The air wooshed from her lungs and her eyes went wide with surprise. Then he got in her face, so close their noses were almost touching.

"I'm going to warn you one last time," he said, teeth clenched, jaw tight. "Do not mess with me or you *will* regret it."

He let go and swiped her shirt from the floor, thrusting it at her. Then he turned and folded his arms across his chest, waiting for her to leave. He heard the rustle of fabric, then the door opened and snapped shut again.

He was almost afraid to turn around. Afraid he'd find her completely naked and undeterred, and this time he might not be able to hold back.

But when he turned, he found the room empty. It wasn't until then that he realized he was shaking.

At 6:00 the following morning, Connor trudged down the stairs, feeling cranky and out of sorts. He'd slept like hell last night, guilt burning a hole in his gut every time he thought of how he'd treated Nita. But she hadn't given him a choice. There hadn't been any other way to get through to her.

He walked into the kitchen, expecting to find her there eating her breakfast, but the room was empty. He checked the office next, but she wasn't there, either, and she wasn't upstairs in her room.

Where the hell was she?

He took the stairs two at a time and headed out to the stable. The sun was a glowing orange shadow on the horizon and the air was chilly and scented with fresh hay.

No Nita, but he did find Jimmy.

"Have you seen Nita?" Connor asked him.

"She got up early this morning. A couple of the men thought they saw a light out in the west pasture last night. They took the truck out there but whoever it was musta heard 'em and run off. Nita went to check it out."

"*Alone, in the dark?*"

The old man shrugged. "Said she wanted to search the property for more holes before we set the horses out to pasture."

Connor could hardly believe what he was hearing. "And you let her go?"

His look was solemn. "She is the boss, Connor. I'm in no position to be giving her orders."

"You could have at least gone with her."

"I offered, she said no thanks."

Connor knew she was doing this to get back at him for last night. He cursed under his breath and headed for

Goliath's stall. He had him saddled and ready to go in three minutes. "She ever does this again, you come and find me right away."

"I know you're worried about her getting hurt, but she can handle herself," Jimmy said as Connor walked Goliath out of the stable and mounted him.

"I know she'd like to believe that, but right now, she's not safe anywhere by herself." He drove his heels into the horse's sides and took off in search of her.

Nita studied the tracks in the dirt. There was a single shovel mark in the ground, as if the digger had been interrupted. That must have been about the time the boys drove out to investigate.

She shook her head. Whoever was doing this, was certainly persistent, and not very intelligent if he thought she would fall for this old trick again. But if he'd set out to annoy her, he'd succeeded. She was going to have to have a talk with the men to see if anyone would be willing to patrol the property at night until the guilty party was caught. Maybe they could take three- or four-hour shifts. And if they were really lucky, maybe they would catch him in the act.

A smile curled her lips when she thought about what she would do if she caught him herself.

She heard the beat of a horse's hooves and, looking at her watch, knew it was Connor. She didn't have to turn and look at him to know he'd be angry she'd left without him.

She was hoping he would be, though it couldn't begin to make up for the anger and humiliation she'd felt last night when he'd turned her down. And yes, she'd been hurt. She'd never misread a man as badly as she had Connor. She'd been sure he was as interested in her as she was in him.

Apparently not.

Although that didn't explain the bulge in his jeans. He'd definitely been turned on, but he sure had freaked out when she'd touched him. Then it occurred to her, maybe by saying he was damaged, he'd meant he was physically disfigured somewhere down there. He had been in an explosion. What if his back wasn't the only place he'd been burned. Maybe he was embarrassed to let her see him.

Oddly enough, the thought was almost comforting. He hadn't actually rejected her. He was looking out for her welfare—protecting her from the gruesome truth. And he'd said that, hadn't he? At the time she'd figured it was just some lame put-down line. Maybe he thought she'd be appalled by the way he looked.

Well, hell, he didn't need to feel embarrassed. She didn't care what it looked like, as long as the plumbing worked, and even if there were kinks to work out she would be okay with that, too. The more challenging, the more fun as far as she was concerned.

Maybe this wasn't a lost cause after all.

Connor stopped a few feet from where she was crouched inspecting the ground. "What the hell do you think you're doing?"

If he was going to go all macho on her, maybe she shouldn't be so eager to let him off the hook. She slowly rose to her feet and turned to him, her face the picture of serenity. "Good morning to you, too."

He jumped down from his horse. "Look, I know you're probably upset about last night…"

Oh yeah, he was askin' for it. "Don't flatter yourself, cowboy. Men like you are a dime a dozen. It's a shame though, we could have had fun."

If she'd wounded his pride, he didn't let it show. "Then why did you leave without me? Are you *trying* to get yourself killed?"

"I have a farm to run. If you can't keep up with me, that's not my problem." She mounted her horse and headed for the stable, Connor riding close behind her, a silent sentinel. He didn't say a word the entire ride, but she could feel his anger hovering over her like a heavy black storm cloud. And she was only slightly enjoying it.

Well, maybe more than slightly.

Jimmy was outside the stable waiting for them.

"Looks like our digger was back," she told him. "I found more holes in the west corral. I want the boys to fill them, then search every inch of the property for more."

"Yes, ma'am."

She hopped down from her horse and headed for the house to see if her daddy was up. They had housekeepers to interview starting at ten.

"When were you planning on telling me about the holes?" Connor asked from behind her. From the tightness in his voice, she could tell he was still angry, but trying hard to hold it in. He'd feel a whole lot better if he just blew up at her and got it out of his system. He was too closed off, too darned controlled all the time.

Knowing she was throwing kindling on the flames, Nita shrugged and said, "You didn't ask."

"I shouldn't have to."

"Look, Connor," she shot over her shoulder. "I don't

have time to babysit you today. Why don't you make yourself useful and go help the men fill the holes?"

"You know I can't do that."

"I'll be perfectly safe in the house with Daddy."

"Your father is in a cast. If someone were to come in and grab you, what would he be able to do to stop them?"

"I don't think someone is going to waltz into the house in the middle of the day."

"It doesn't matter what you think," he said, his voice so tight she'd bet that given one good pluck, his vocal cords would snap in two.

She could see there was no reasoning with him. Not that she'd *ever* been able to reason with him, so it wasn't a big surprise. And boy, he was cranky today. Probably sexual frustration, she decided. If he had just given in last night, after she was through with him, he'd have slept like a baby.

He followed her in the back door, through the mudroom, and into the kitchen. Her father was at the table eating a bowl of cold cereal.

"Morning, Daddy, how do you feel?"

He slammed his spoon down on the table. "I'm sick of cold cereal, that's how I feel. When are those housekeepers coming?"

Jeez, was everyone in a foul mood this morning? "The first one is coming at ten."

"How many answered the ad?"

"Only two."

"Only *two*?"

Nita shrugged. "People talk. Everyone knows what's been happening out here. Can you blame someone for not wanting to get involved? Maybe we should try advertising in other cities." Or just call Jane, she wanted to add.

He muttered something about "Those damned Devlins" then boosted himself on his crutches and hobbled out of the room.

Nita hoped the interview process was only a formality, and that her daddy would come to his senses and ask Jane to come home soon. Nita figured it was just a matter of time before he missed Jane so much he would be begging her to return.

"I talked to my brother last night," Connor said from his spot near the door. He didn't look angry anymore. Just mildly annoyed. "Jake would like to bring the map by tonight about seven."

"Map?"

"The one that was stolen from the museum," he reminded her. "The one Gavin wanted me to look at."

"Oh, right. Fine by me," she said.

"I also talked to Clint about the security evaluation and he said he'd be by around three, day after tomorrow."

"Not that I think this evaluation will do much good, but I'll listen to what he has to say." She cleared her daddy's breakfast dishes and carried them to the sink.

"Nita, about last night…"

Not this again. Sheesh. Rub it in my face why don't you. She leaned on the edge of the sink. "You don't have to explain. I get it."

"I just want to make it clear, it wasn't you."

"I understand. You were embarrassed. It's okay."

His eyebrow dipped low. "Embarrassed?"

"About your condition."

"Condition?" Connor folded his arms across his

chest, wondering what the hell she was talking about now. "And what *condition* might that be."

Her eyes drifted to the vicinity of his crotch. "The damage."

He couldn't tell if she was serious, or just yanking his chain. "What damage are we talking about?"

"From the explosion. I understand why you're afraid to let me see it. But you should know, I wouldn't be bothered by any…abnormalities. I mean, penises are pretty funny looking to begin with, so how bad could it be?"

"Nita, what are you talking about? Why would you assume any part of my anatomy is abnormal?"

"I'm not assuming anything. You said so yourself last night."

"When?"

"You said your goods were damaged."

He nearly laughed out loud. Leave it to her to twist his words into something so totally off the wall. He might have been offended if he wasn't so damned amused. "Nita, trust me when I say my goods are just fine."

She shrugged and walked past him, through the kitchen doorway, calling over her shoulder, "Hey, whatever you say."

He followed her down the hall and into the office. "What, you don't believe me?"

She crossed the room and sat in the chair behind her wide, cluttered oak desk. "Connor, you have nothing to be ashamed of."

"You're right, I don't. Because there's nothing wrong with me."

She flipped open her laptop. "So you've said."

She was goading him now, and he was having too

much fun not to play along for a while. To see exactly what she thought she might accomplish by antagonizing him. Though he already had a pretty good idea.

She needed justification. She needed to know why he'd rejected her. What she'd done wrong.

And the answer was nothing. She done everything right. He was the one with the problem. If only she knew how difficult it had been for him to turn her away last night, how much he still wanted her. He had no idea how she'd made it this far in life thinking that she wasn't feminine, that she looked like a boy. She had to be one of the most desirable, sexiest women he'd ever met. The kind of woman he typically avoided at all cost, which was a little tough to do living in the same house, shadowing her every move.

"You know," she said, thoughtfully. "They have some wonderful new drugs out to help men with certain… problems."

He swallowed a grin. "Not only am I deformed, now I'm impotent, too?"

"I'm only telling you so you don't think it's hopeless. There is help out there for men like you."

"What was it you said last night? Everything seems to be working fine?"

She let out a long, gusty sigh and rolled the chair back from the desk. "If you're so determined to convince me I'm wrong, I guess I'll just have to see it."

Somehow he knew it would come to this. "You will, huh?"

"Drop your pants. Let's have a look." She propped her elbows on the armrests and linked her fingers under her chin—the picture of solemnity, but there was no mistaking that impish gleam in her eye. "Come on, don't be shy. I promise I won't laugh."

No, he knew she wouldn't laugh. He didn't even want to think of what she might do if she got him out of his pants. But whatever it was, he was sure she'd do it well.

He propped his hands on the desk and leaned forward, looking her right in the eye, so there was no mistaking what he was about to tell her. "I like you, Nita. Too much. Which is exactly why I can't get involved with you. There's a lot that you don't know about me."

She held his gaze. "Does that mean you won't be taking off your pants?"

"No, I won't."

She shrugged and rolled her chair up to her computer. "Then get lost, I have work to do."

"So we understand each other?"

"Yes, Connor. We understand each other. Personally, I think you're blowing this whole sex thing *way* out of proportion, but I guess it's your loss." She made a shooing gesture with her hands. "Now go 'way. I have things to do before the applicants get here."

"I'll be on my bench in the foyer if you need me," he said, then headed for the door. He glanced back on his way out and saw that she was mesmerized by whatever she was working on.

She'd been awfully agreeable about the whole thing. *Too* agreeable. He couldn't escape the feeling that he hadn't heard the last of this.

Seven

"It's sort of pretty," Nita said, running her fingers across the photocopy of the map, over scores of tiny hearts, all different shapes and sizes. "What do they mean?"

"That's what we're trying to figure out," Gavin said. He stood between her and Jake.

Connor stood across from them on the other side of the kitchen table. He'd been keeping his distance all day. Not that he wasn't still following her everywhere, he'd just been doing it from a couple yards away.

He was a tough one to figure out. She'd told him she didn't want commitment, and still he'd turned her down, even though he was obviously attracted to her—because there were things about him she didn't know. Well, heck, there were things about her he didn't know, either. They didn't have to be best buddies to enjoy each other's…company. As far as she was concerned, it was better that they weren't. She didn't like it when men got attached to her. That was right about the time they started trying to change her, to mold her into something she didn't want to be. Something she *couldn't* be.

He thought he had issues? Well, who didn't? That shouldn't stop them from having fun.

"We've been looking for some sort of pattern," Jake told Nita. "But so far we've come up empty."

There was a time, when she first met Connor, that she'd thought Jake was the more attractive of the two. His stunning smile and cheerful disposition were hard to resist. But there was something about Connor, something dark and exciting, that intrigued her.

And the more Connor eluded her, the more frustrated she grew. Maybe it was the thrill of the chase, but she'd never wanted a man the way she wanted him. It felt almost like an obsession. Getting in his pants was all she seemed to think about anymore, and at the same time, it wasn't about sex.

She didn't know what it was about anymore.

"There doesn't seem to be any rhyme or reason to it," Gavin said. "If we knew the location of the land, it might make more sense. All we know is that it's somewhere in Royal."

"We thought maybe Connor would recognize some of the markings," Jake added.

Connor shook his head. "Sorry. It's like nothing I've ever seen before."

"It looks old," Nita said.

"Jessamine Golden disappeared shortly after the turn of the last century," Jake told her, "making the map at least one hundred years old. Most of the landmarks could be long gone by now. It could be next to impossible to determine its location."

"Let me have a look at that." Her daddy hobbled in from the living room on his crutches. "I've lived in Royal my whole life, maybe I'll recognize the land."

Jake and Gavin nodded and Connor stepped aside so Will could take a look.

Her daddy studied it for all of about two seconds when his brow furrowed and he asked, "You fellas aren't pulling my leg now, are you?"

"What do you mean?" Nita asked.

"I mean, is this some kinda joke?"

"You recognize it?" Connor asked.

"Well, of course I do. This here is Windcroft land."

Nita looked at the map again and shook her head. "But Daddy, that's too big to be Windcroft land."

"But it used be bigger," Connor reminded her.

"Before the Devlins stole it from us," her daddy added bitterly. "I reckon this map was drawn up before the poker game."

Nita looked over at Connor. "Are you telling me that all that gold is buried *here?*"

Connor smacked himself in the forehead. "All this time it was staring us right in the face. I can't believe I didn't figure it out before."

"Figure what out?" Jake asked.

"All the holes dug on the property."

"Oh my gosh," Nita said, the truth knocking her for a loop. "They weren't dug to hurt the horses after all. Someone was looking for buried treasure!"

"And I'll bet that gold is the reason that someone has been trying to get you off the land," Connor said.

"But who?" Gavin asked.

"Jonathan Devlin had this map," Will said. "And he would have recognized the land, too. Probably every one of the Devlins knows about it."

"But do they know which heart marks the treasure?"

"Considering all the holes we found," Nita said, "they don't have a clue."

"There's so many of them," Will said. "It could be anywhere. In the corrals, under the stables or the house. It could take years to find it."

"And we still don't know who's doing the digging," Nita added.

"But we're getting closer," Jake said, rolling the map. "Connor, could Gavin and I have a word with you?"

"Nita, would you mind if we use the office?" Connor asked.

"Of course not," she said.

"Wait for me here," he told her, his tone threatening enough to let her know he meant business.

She saluted him. "Yes, sir."

Shaking his head, Connor led his brother and Gavin into the office, switched the light on and closed the door. "What's up?"

"We just wondered how things are going out here," Jake said. "If you've found any evidence linking Nita to Jonathan Devlin's murder."

"Nita is a lot of things, but she's not a murderer. Alison is right, she's not capable."

Jake grinned. "Is that your personal or professional opinion?"

He shot his brother a look.

"She is awfully cute," Jake taunted.

Gavin laughed. "If she ever heard you call her that, I'll bet you'd be nursing a black eye. She doesn't strike me as the type who would appreciate men referring to her as *cute*."

"Does she know why you're really here?" Jake asked.

"Yeah, she knows," Connor grumbled, and she sure as hell hadn't been making his job easy. Twice that day he'd taken his eyes off her for about half a second, and when he turned around, she was gone. She was stealthy as a cat and twice as obstinate. She was going to fool around and get herself hurt.

That gold was worth millions. If it really was buried somewhere on their property as the map indicated, who knows to what lengths the people searching for it would go to get their hands on it.

"By your tone, am I to assume she's giving you trouble?" Jake asked.

"From what I hear, trouble is her middle name," Gavin said.

Connor snorted. "That's an understatement."

"At least we know for certain that someone else is responsible for the problems out here," Gavin said. "And we know why."

"But is it the Devlins?" Jake wanted to know.

"Tom called me today saying he had new information about the feud," Gavin told them. "Rumor has it that about four weeks after Jonathan died, his grandson Lucas, Tom's uncle, approached Will Windcroft in the Royal Diner. Witnesses heard Lucas saying something about the two of them needing to talk, but Will got angry and stormed out of the restaurant. Tom was supposed to have a meeting with Lucas to try to find out what it was he needed to talk about."

"Maybe it'll be the answer we're looking for," Jake said.

"I'm hoping it is. He wants us to meet at the club tomorrow afternoon. Can you make it, Connor?"

"Nita mentioned driving into town for supplies. We can bring Jimmy, the stable manager, along to keep an eye on her. She should be safe with him while I come to the club."

They agreed on 3:00 p.m. and Connor walked them out to their cars. Jake hung back and, after Gavin had driven away, he asked, "So, what do you think of her?"

"Who?"

"You know who."

Yeah, Connor did, and he didn't want to talk about it. "It's a job."

"There's chemistry there."

It wasn't a question, and even if it had been, Connor couldn't deny it. And he *still* didn't want to talk about it.

"I knew there would be. It's part of the reason I recommended you for the job."

What was he, some kind of matchmaker now? "Well, you were wasting your time."

"You know, Connor, it wouldn't kill you to relax and have some fun for a change. Do something for yourself."

"You would know a lot about that," Connor said, regretting his harsh tone the second the words left his mouth. He wasn't being fair. Jake had changed. And he'd proven that in his race for mayor.

Jake being Jake, the insult slid right off his back. "Connor, you'd be amazed what finding the right woman can do to a man."

There was no right woman for Connor. And even if he found her, it simply couldn't be. He had too much anger, too much rage. He could try to explain, but Jake would never understand. They might look alike, but inside they couldn't be more different.

The truth was, Connor wished he were more like his brother.

"I'll see you tomorrow at three," Connor said, opening Jakes car door.

Taking Connor's not so subtle hint, Jake grinned and got inside. "I'll see you tomorrow."

Connor watched him drive away, until his taillights were two red specks in the blackness of the night, then he went in the house to find Nita and tell her about tomorrow's meeting. Will was in the family room watching a football game.

"Where's Nita?"

Will barely glanced up at Connor, his attention rooted to the television. "She went out to the stable for something. Said you could meet her out there."

Connor closed his eyes and cursed under his breath. She'd done it again. She'd completely ignored what he'd assumed was a pretty direct order. And by doing so, had once again put herself in danger. She didn't seem to understand how serious this situation had become.

Anger shooting his blood pressure into the red zone, Connor stomped his way through the kitchen and mudroom out into the night. The sky was overcast and black as pitch. It was so dark the back porch light barely lit his way to the stable. From the bunkhouse he could hear laughter and music and warm light glowed behind the curtains.

The main stable was dark.

She's in there, perfectly safe, he told himself. She'd only left the lights off to scare him. That's what he had to believe, because the alternative wasn't even worth considering.

He pulled the door open and stepped inside, his eyes taking a second to adjust to the dim light, relief washing over him when he saw Nita. Relief that quickly dissolved into anger.

She stood in front of Goliath's stall, illuminated only by the lamp burning on the desk in the stable office. Soft light surrounded her, making her hair shimmer as she moved, making her skin look soft and translucent. She looked...beautiful. If he hadn't been so damned mad, it would have taken his breath away.

"So, this is how it's going to be," he said. "You slipping away from me whenever I'm not looking?"

She ran a brush down the side of the horse's neck. "I like to come out here at night. It's peaceful. It helps me think."

"And it's dangerous."

"I'm all right, aren't I?"

"Do you have any idea what's at stake here? I've seen what people will do for money, the lengths they'll go to. That gold is worth millions, and someone is after it. Right now you're the only thing standing in their way."

"I refuse to be a victim. To be afraid in my own home." She turned to face him and for a moment he was taken aback. She may have sounded confident and downright belligerent, but he could see genuine concern in her eyes. And fear. Their discovery tonight had obviously ruffled her more than she'd let on, and the anger he'd been feeling slipped.

"You don't have to be a victim, but you do have to be smart," he said, suddenly feeling sorry for her. She was so tough, so burdened with responsibility, he wondered if she ever allowed herself to let it all go. To be vulnerable.

Somehow he doubted it.

"We can't let word out that the gold is here," she said. "We'll have every kook in the county trying to find it. And what if it's all a ruse? What if that map is some kind of red herring?"

As he drew closer to her, his body came alive with awareness. He couldn't be in the same room without getting caught up in her scent, without being mesmerized by the way her body moved. "I have a meeting tomorrow to discuss the feud. It seems there have been new developments. Maybe it will help us to figure out who's responsible."

"I just want this to be over before our business is ruined," she said, frustration keen in her voice. She turned to hang the brush back on its hook, but not before he could see the stark sadness on her face. His first instinct was to pull her into his arms and just hold her. To give her the freedom to let go.

He stepped up behind her and laid his hands over her shoulders, realizing instantly that touching her had been a mistake. The contact shot through him like jolt of pure energy. But by then it was too late. The second he touched her, Nita turned and pressed herself against him. His arms naturally went around her, holding her close. He had never imagined that something as simple as holding a woman could feel so damned good. So... erotic. He was hyperaware of every inch of her supple figure, the body heat that seeped though her clothes.

Instead of pulling away, he let his cheek rest against the softness of her hair. He wanted to tangle his fingers through it, tilt her head and kiss her. Take everything he'd never let himself take from a woman and give it all back in return.

Nita's hands flattened against his back and began to drift slowly downward. She pressed her face against his chest, her breath hot through his shirt. He could tell by her increased breathing, by the way her body went from rigid and tense to soft and pliable, she was just as aroused.

Then he felt her breath on his neck, her lips on his throat. He had to stop this. He had to end it before they went too far, before they reached the point of no return. What had made him think he could touch her this way without wanting more?

"Don't do that," he croaked, barely able to push the words out, to contain the desire building inside of him.

"Why? I know you want me to." Her hands cupped his backside, and she arched against him. "I can feel how much."

"I'll hurt you, Nita. Even if I don't want to."

Her teeth scraped his earlobe and he fisted his hands to keep from caressing her. "Have I ever once given you the impression that I can't fend for myself?"

Why couldn't she listen? Why couldn't she see the mistake she was making? "Not from me you can't."

"You're not nearly as tough as you think."

She ran her tongue along the seam of his ear and it was more than he could take. He grabbed her by the shoulders and pushed her away.

"I don't know how else to say this to you, Nita. I'm *not* interested."

For a second she looked stunned, then her eyes darkened with anger. "You wouldn't know what to do with a woman if she walked up and bit you."

"When you see one, you let me know."

Her jaw clenched tight and her eyes reduced to slits and he knew he'd hit a nerve. That was good, because when she was angry with him, she wasn't thinking of ways to seduce him. All those wicked ideas she seemed to have would only get her in trouble. It would get them *both* in trouble.

But she was so wrong. He knew exactly what he wanted to do with her.

She spun on her heel and headed for the door, but not before he saw something else in her eyes. He saw hurt. He'd wounded her pride, and he didn't figure that was an easy thing to do.

He felt like slime for it, because he'd made her believe that he didn't want her, that she wasn't beautiful and sexy and everything any man could ever hope to find in a woman. Himself included.

"Nita, wait." She was all the way to the stable door before he caught up with her. He grabbed her arm, stopping her in her tracks. She flung herself around, her eyes two purple balls of fire in the dim light.

"Get your hands off me." She spit out a stream of curses even he'd never used then she shoved him. Hard. So hard he stumbled backward and almost landed on his rear end.

Blood pulsed through his veins and throbbed at his temple. She had no idea what she was doing, what he was capable of. "Don't do that again."

"What's the matter?" she asked, taking a step toward him, her chin high. "You don't like being pushed around by a girl."

"Stop it, Nita," he warned through clenched teeth, but his threat only fueled her determination.

"What are you going to do about it?" She stepped up to him, planted her hands on his chest and shoved again, harder this time, and his blood pressure reached an all-new high. She could see how angry he was, but instead of being afraid, instead of looking wary, she looked even more excited, more determined.

"I'm warning you," he said, "don't do that again."

With her eyes locked on his, taunting him, she very deliberately planted her hands on his chest, ready to give him another good hard shove.

All the anger, all the frustration he'd trapped deep below the surface broke free in a red-hot gush. Before he could stop himself, he caught her wrists in his hands and backed her hard against the door, pinning her arms over her head. He wanted to hurt her, and he wanted scare her and he just plain wanted her, as he'd never wanted a woman before.

She gazed up at him through the pale light, but instead of looking frightened, instead of being angry with him, her lids were heavy with desire, her cheeks flushed.

Before he even knew what he was doing, he lowered his head and crushed his mouth to hers—a hard, punishing kiss—pressing her to the door with the weight of his body. Her mouth was hot and sweet and demanding, her body soft and needy.

He lost himself in the flavor of her mouth, the thrust

of her tongue against his own. His hands slipped from her wrists and found their way to the curve of her hips, down the swell of her backside, and Nita moaned into his mouth. Her arms wound around his neck and she hooked one leg over his hip, grinding her body against him.

That's when he started to melt, when the last of his control began to slip. He began to feel—as he'd never felt before. Arousal and lust and longing. It overwhelmed him.

And scared the hell out of him.

He pried her arms from around his neck and backed away, drawing a hand across his damp mouth, fighting to catch his breath. "Now you see what you've done?"

"You say that like it's a bad thing." She looked like pure sex standing there, her chest heaving, her cheeks the same vivid red as the stripes on her shirt. It was almost more than he could take.

"I'm not doing this with you, Nita. No matter how much we both want it."

She studied him for a long moment and something in her eyes told him she knew it was a lost cause.

"That's a fine attitude, now that you've gotten me all hot and bothered," she said, her voice low and husky.

"I sincerely apologize."

"No need to apologize." She flattened a hand over her chest where her collar opened, then slipped it inside, caressing the top of her breast, her eyes pinned on his. "Guess I'll just have to go upstairs and take care of business myself."

She gave her breast a squeeze and he nearly fell over. It would take the willpower of ten men not to pull her back into his arms, yet somehow he managed all by himself. But she wasn't finished with him. As she opened the door to leave, she dealt the blow that nearly brought him to his knees.

"Later, when you're lying in bed and you hear me cry out from the next room, know that it's you I was thinking about."

Eight

Connor sat in a leather arm chair in the cigar lounge of the Cattleman's Club, head resting on his fisted hand, struggling to stay awake. Figuring Nita would make good on her threat last night in the stable, Connor had slept sitting up on the bench in the foyer. Far enough away that he couldn't hear her *cry out,* as she'd put it, but where he could catch her if she tried to sneak down the stairs and give him the slip again—which she had, at 5:45 that morning. And though he'd slept in far worse conditions in the Rangers, sheer sexual frustration had kept him awake most of the night. That and his own self-doubt.

He couldn't stop thinking about what his brother had said, about what the right woman could do to a man, and how Connor needed to do something for himself. It was true that, since he'd been away from the engineering firm, since he'd started working the farm with Nita, he'd lost that feeling of restlessness, the bone-deep frustration he always seemed to feel whenever he let himself take a step back and look good and hard at his life. That frustration had always been the catalyst, the trigger for the irrepressible rage.

Not that he hadn't felt frustration lately, but this was an entirely different variety. It was born from the need to keep Nita safe, from her constant refusal to listen to him. From the affection and attraction that he knew was wrong, and felt despite that.

Every so often he'd felt a flicker of something else, too. An emotion he hadn't experienced in so long he'd barely recognized it.

He'd felt content.

Not that he expected it to last. It never did.

Jake dropped into the chair next to his. "You look like hell."

Connor shot him an annoyed look. "Thanks."

"Being a newlywed, I have a valid reason for being up half the night. What's your excuse? Don't tell me you turned her down."

The look went from annoyed to deadly.

Jake laughed. "I don't understand why you're fighting it. You two are meant for each other."

"How could you possibly know that?"

"Because I know Nita and I know you. She needs someone who won't be threatened by her strength, someone who won't try to change her, and you need someone who can show you how to have fun. I would say that makes you a perfect match."

If what his brother was saying made a weird sort of sense, Connor wrote it off as the direct result of sleep deprivation. He knew he was loopy when the next question popped from his mouth. "What did you mean about what finding the right woman can do to a man?"

"Something just…clicks. You start to look at things differently, to see yourself differently. Your priorities change."

"But you must have dated a hundred different women. How did you know Chris was the one?"

"It was the freckles," Jake said with that goofy grin of his. "I'm a sucker for that woman's freckles."

"Freckles?" Leave it to Jake to give him such a ridiculous answer.

"In time, you'll know exactly what I mean." He slugged Connor in the arm, then got up to talk to Gavin, leaving Connor even more confused than he'd been before.

"Since we're all here we should get started," Tom said. Connor looked to the doorway and saw that Mark, just back from his honeymoon, had arrived. "I talked to my uncle Lucas yesterday. It took some persuading, but I finally got him to admit what he'd planned to tell Will Windcroft.

"It seems that after his grandfather, Jonathan, was killed, and my uncle was going through his things, he noticed some odd notations in his personal bookkeeping and large payments Jonathan had been receiving from an unknown source."

"What are we talking about?" Gavin asked. "Extortion?"

"Lucas said his grandfather was a greedy bastard and was definitely capable of blackmail."

"So, if we find out who he was blackmailing, we'll most likely find his killer."

"He also found letters to Jonathan. They were vague, but one mentioned a payment and a diary and how there could be trouble if the Windcrofts ever found out. Another talked of keeping the feud going."

"Were the letters from someone in the Devlin family?" Logan wanted to know.

"I asked. Lucas said they weren't signed, and there was no return address on the envelopes, but he was under the impression they were from someone outside the family."

Gavin sipped his drink. "Meaning someone outside the Devlin family could have a stake in the feud, and has a reason for keeping it going. Do we have any idea who that could be? Or where this diary is?"

"No," Tom said. "But if we find it, I get the feeling we'll have all the answers we're looking for."

"And Lucas never told any of this to Will?" Connor asked.

"Lucas wanted to come clean with Will, but when Will refused to talk to him he felt stung. I believe he honestly wants to bring an end to the feud."

"I could talk to Will," Connor offered.

Tom shook his head. "I think it would be better coming from me. From a Devlin. But before I do, I'd like to dig a bit more and see what I can find. Some undisputed proof would make convincing him a lot easier."

Gavin stood and set down his glass. "While you're doing that, the rest of us will ask around about this diary and keep looking for the people causing the Windcrofts trouble. Have there been any more problems at the farm, Connor?"

"We found more holes yesterday morning. Nita has a man watching the property at night. I've instructed the hands to call me on my cell if they see anything suspicious. Until we know who we're dealing with, I don't want them trying to apprehend anyone."

"Keep us posted on the situation and we'll keep digging."

When the meeting was over Connor called Nita to let her know he was ready to be picked up. She informed him curtly that she and Jimmy were shopping for groceries and she would be there when she was good and ready. All the way into town she and Jimmy had chatted while she'd ignored Connor. He figured she was still ticked off that she hadn't been able to sneak away from him that morning. She also was growing increasingly frustrated with the fact that they had no housekeeper. Her father had shot down the two candidates they'd interviewed yesterday, saying they just weren't right, and no one else had answered the ad.

Nita seemed to be at the end of her rope.

It was the middle of a workday and the club was fairly quiet, so Connor decided he might as well get some shut-eye while he waited. He walked back to the cigar lounge and made himself comfortable in a soft leather chair in the corner. He'd trained himself to sleep lightly in the Rangers, so when he heard the door open, heard the muffled sound of footsteps coming in his direction, he was only half-asleep.

Nita kicked his boot. "Wake up."

He opened his eyes.

She hovered over him, hands on her hips, Stetson pulled low over her eyes.

"How did you get in here?" he asked.

A wry smile curled her mouth. "The staff here learned the hard way not to mess with me. I think they hide when they see me comin'."

"Can't say I blame them."

Her grin widened. Apparently she wasn't angry with him any longer. "You ready to go?"

"Yeah, I'm ready."

He pulled himself from the chair and followed her out to the truck. Jimmy was leaning against the passenger door waiting for them and the bed was filled with groceries and supplies.

"You tell him?" Jimmy asked.

Nita shot Connor a nervous look. "I told you, there's nothing to tell. It was an accident."

No wonder she was being so nice. She was hiding something from him. He should have known. "What was an accident?"

Jimmy ignored Nita's warning look. "Me and Nita were on Main Street waiting to cross and a car came out of nowhere and nearly ran her down."

Connor swore under his breath.

"I'm sure it was just an accident," Nita said hastily. "No one would try to run someone down in the middle of a busy street on purpose."

"If they were desperate to get rid of you they might," Connor said. "What type of car was it?"

"It happened so fast I didn't get a good look," Jimmy said. "I'm pretty sure it was a black BMW. Maybe dark blue. Not much help considering half of Royal drives those."

"You didn't see the license place?"

Jimmy shook his head. "Happened too fast. By the time I heard Nita swear, and turned to see what had happened, the car was around the corner."

Connor turned to Nita. "Exactly what happened?"

"The light changed, I started to cross, then this car came out of nowhere and shot through the light and turned right. I'm sure it was accidental and they just didn't see me there."

"Could you see the driver?"

"Like Jimmy said, it happened so fast. And the windows were tinted."

Connor didn't like the sound of this. He felt guilty for not being with her. He never should have taken his eyes off her. "Did anyone else see it? Did someone take down the license plate?"

"Why would they?" she snapped. "I told you it was an accident."

No, he didn't think it was an accident at all. If this person was bold enough to try to run her down on a busy street corner, things were even worse than he'd thought.

Nita stuck her head out the bedroom door and peered down the hall. Connor's door was closed, meaning he'd gone to bed.

Too bad for him.

The grandfather clock in the office chimed twelve times as she tiptoed down the darkened hall toward the stairs, careful to avoid the creaky spot just above the top step. Since almost getting run over two days ago—which she was still convinced was an accident—Connor had been stuck to her like glue. She couldn't use the bathroom without him hovering outside the door. And he must have made some sort of pact with the men, because whenever Connor wasn't around, Jimmy or one of the hands kept her in their sights. She realized, in retrospect, that by continually trying to give him the slip, she'd probably only made things worse for herself. But she was beginning to feel smothered, and all she really wanted was a few blissful minutes to herself. Even if that meant just sitting on the swing and looking at the stars, which is exactly what she planned to do tonight.

She didn't doubt someone was trying to scare them off the land, but besides the holes—which they now knew weren't dug with the intention of hurting anyone—nothing had been done to put her or the staff in danger. Even the letters had been vague. Just your basic *get off the land or else*. Whoever penned them never specified what the *or else* would be if the Windcrofts didn't comply. And here they were, still safe and sound on the land.

She crept across the wood floor to the front door and flipped the deadbolt, cringing as the click echoed through the foyer. She was reaching for the doorknob when a hand clamped down firmly over her shoulder. She let out a shriek of surprise and spun around, and was greeted by the deep baritone of Connor's laughter.

"Are you trying to scare me half to death?" she admonished.

Through the dark she could see he was grinning. "Just making sure you don't sneak away."

"I wasn't sneaking," she lied.

"Uh-huh. That would explain why you were tiptoeing down the stairs." He took in her tennis shoes, flannel pants and University of Texas sweatshirt. "Let me guess, you were sleepwalking?"

"I couldn't sleep. I needed some fresh air to clear my head. I was going to sit on the swing."

He pulled the door open and held it for her. "Let's go."

"*Alone,* Connor. If I wanted company, I would have woken you."

"You have two choices. We can sit out on the swing together, or go back to bed."

"Can we go back to bed together?" she asked, for the mere pleasure of teasing him, because she already knew the answer was no. And of course there was always that million-to-one chance she would catch him in the right mood and he would throw her against the wall, as he'd done in the stable, and ravage her.

"In or out," he said.

And apparently tonight wasn't going to be the night. She sighed and said, "Since I'm up and dressed we might as well go out there."

They walked onto the porch and he pulled the door closed behind them, then followed her down the steps and across the yard to the swing. The air carried a deep chill and dew soaked through the canvas of her shoes. The moon hung low in the sky casting a pale, eerie light across the land.

Nita plopped down in the middle of the swing seat, so that whichever side he chose, Connor would be right next to her. She thought he might complain, instead he sat beside her—so close that their thighs were touching—and draped his arm over the back of the swing behind her shoulders. He pushed off with his foot and they swayed gently back and forth.

"Out of curiosity, how did you know I was coming out here?" she asked.

He leaned his head back and gazed up at the sky. "I heard you moving around in your room. Then I followed you downstairs."

And here she thought *she'd* been so quiet. "What did you do, levitate? I didn't even hear you."

"Don't feel bad. It's what I was trained to do."

"Did you have to kill people, too?"

Through the dark she could see him frown. "Sometimes."

"Jake said you served in the Middle East."

He nodded.

"Is that where you were shot?"

"Yep."

She waited for him to elaborate, but he didn't. "And you apparently don't like to talk about it."

The frown deepened. "The things I saw there, you wouldn't want to know about. Things I wish even I could forget."

He hadn't revealed much, but she felt closer to him somehow, as if he'd exposed a part of himself no one else had ever seen. A part of her wanted to jump off the swing and do a happy dance, while another part warned her to back off. She didn't want to care if he confided in her or not. She was getting too close.

Even when she was angry and frustrated with him, she couldn't be near Connor without experiencing a giddy, excited sensation in her tummy. A need to touch him. To be touched. It was as intriguing as it was frustrating.

She didn't know what it was about him that fascinated her so. She only knew that she wanted—no *needed*—to be near him. She wished he would just give in so their affair could run its course and she could stop feeling this way. She'd been so restless lately, so unfocussed and out of her element. It was as if her entire life was spinning out of control and he was the only thing keeping her rooted in reality. The only thing she could depend on, even if that meant depending on him to constantly avoid her advances.

And she didn't like it one bit.

She shivered under her sweatshirt and Connor surprised her when he slipped his arm from the swing onto her shoulder.

"Cold?"

"A little. It's chillier than I thought it would be."

Well, this was nice. Unexpected, but nice. She inched a little closer and rested her head on his shoulder. The stubble on his chin was rough against her forehead and, Lord, did he smell good. That masculine, woodsy smell that made her want to bury her nose against his neck and sniff. Of course, she knew she couldn't get that close to his neck without taking a nibble or two.

"I know what we could do to raise my body temperature," she said, and heard him chuckle.

"You don't give up easily, do you?"

"I'm not going to fall in love with you if that's what you're worried about. I know a lot of women say that but don't really mean it. I'm too independent for that. I just want us to have some fun."

"It's not that I don't want to, Nita. It's too risky."

Too risky? What was that supposed to mean? "Are you afraid I'm going to get pregnant or something? Do you think I have diseases?"

"It has nothing to do with that."

"Is it my age? Do you think I'm too young? Too immature?"

He turned his head, brushed his lips across her hair. "Nope, you're just right."

She could feel how much he wanted her, could see it in his eyes every time he looked at her. Why wouldn't he just give in to the inevitable? "Would you please explain to me exactly what the problem is? I'm getting a complex here."

He was quiet for several minutes and she could practically feel him working it out in his head, deciding what to tell her. Finally he said, "I have a temper, Nita."

She snorted. "Tell me something I didn't already know. I have a temper, too. So what?"

"Sometimes I don't have a lot of control over it. And when I get really angry, bad things happen."

"What kinds of things?"

"Things I don't want to talk about."

She reached up, touched his cheek. "I'm not afraid of you, Connor."

"You should be." He grabbed her hand and held it, gazed down at her. "All my life, the only way I've been able to control my temper is to keep a tight rein on my emotions. But when I'm with you, when you touch me, I feel like I have no control at all."

Instead of feeling fearful, a shiver of excitement raced through her. She wanted to make him lose control. Wanted to push him to feel everything he wouldn't allow himself to feel. "It's okay to lose control sometimes."

The arm around her tightened. "Not for me."

She could feel herself being pulled in emotionally, sinking too deeply into a relationship that should have been anything but. Yet she couldn't stop it. She had to know.

"Tell me," she said, looking up at him, disturbed by the anguish in his eyes, by the raw hurt. "Tell me what happened to make you feel this way. Why you don't trust yourself?"

"Because I almost killed a man with my bare hands."

Nine

"**W**ho was it?" Nita asked.

Connor didn't want to do this. Didn't want her to know who he really was, but there was no other way to make her understand. No other way for her to see the mistake she was making. "He was in my platoon. One of my men. A friend."

"What happened?"

He leaned his head back against the swing and gazed up at the stars, at the same sky he'd gazed up at that night. It felt like yesterday, and it felt like a hundred years ago. "He used to be one of my best men, but he'd changed those last few months. The things we saw over there..." He shook his head. "He'd become reckless, self-destructive. I didn't realize how bad it was and I kept cutting him slack. I thought that whatever was wrong with him, he would work through it. But that night he disobeyed a direct order. He disclosed our location and put us all in mortal danger."

"Is that when you were shot?"

"Me and half a dozen other men were injured. Two almost fatally. I've always had a volatile temper, but that night, I lost it. It took four men to pull me off him."

"Everyone has a breaking point," she told him. "He'd pushed you too far."

"And I should have taken formal action against him. Instead I flew into a rage. If they hadn't pulled me off, I wouldn't have stopped. I would have killed him."

"But you didn't."

"But I would have, and the worst part, the thing that makes me sick to my stomach, is when I went back a few weeks ago they threw a damned party for me. This man who I nearly beat to death came up to me and apologized. Said he was sorry he let me down."

"He respects you," she said.

"I gave him no reason to."

Nita stroked his arm, and the simple gesture took away some of the pain. Soothed him in a way he'd never felt soothed before. He was so tired of feeling angry. So sick of the guilt. But it wouldn't go away. It was as if it had become an extension of his personality. A part of his soul.

"This is why you left the army, isn't it?"

"I had to. What if I lose it like that again? Next time, someone might not be there to stop me."

She was quiet for several minutes. He needed her to tell him that it was over, that she would stop pursuing him. He both anticipated and dreaded it.

"Connor," she finally said, turning to face him. "Were you happy in the army?"

Her question threw him. "What do you mean?"

"I mean, did you enjoy it?"

"I was serving my country."

"Yes, I realize that. But did you like it?"

It was what he was meant to do. What he was expected to do. Whether or not he liked it had never crossed his mind. "It was an honorable career," he told her.

She blew out a frustrated breath. "Let's try this again. When you were in the army, did you have fun?"

"It's not supposed to be fun."

"Yes, Connor, it *is*. When I wake up in the morning, I can't wait to get to work because I love it. Sometimes, when I'm training a horse, it's scary and it's frustrating and it's difficult, and it's still *fun*." She touched his cheek, turned his head so he would look at her. "I'm going to ask you again, did you enjoy being in the army?"

"It's what was expected of me. What I was good at."

"What about working in your father's firm. Is that fun?"

He gave a rueful laugh. "I don't think you could ever categorize engineering as fun."

"The people who like to do it can. The people who don't do it because it's what is expected of them."

"Life is not about having fun."

"Why not? Shouldn't it be?"

Good question. One he'd never considered—and had no idea how to answer.

She didn't wait for one. "If you're not having fun, you're most likely unhappy, and people who aren't happy get angry and bitter. And if they don't do anything to change, they just get angrier and angrier until they snap."

It took a full minute for his brain to absorb the meaning of her words, the concept was so foreign to him. Could she be right? Could his rage, his anger be the result of a life spent pleasing other people? Had he really been so unhappy?

What was it his brother had said? Connor needed someone who could show him how to have fun. Had he become so closed off, so mired in other people's expectations and his father's constant disapproval, that he'd forgotten how to have fun?

Hell, had he *ever* known? Had he *ever* been happy?

Nita yawned and stretched, and pulled herself to her feet. "Well, it's getting late. I think I'll head back up to bed now."

"I'll be up in a bit," he said. He didn't feel much like sleeping.

"You know, you're still welcome to join me."

Everything in him wanted to accept her offer. But he wasn't prepared to drag her into this mess that had become his life.

"Maybe another time," she said, when he didn't answer. "And think about what I said."

Thinking about what she'd said seemed to be all he could do as she disappeared into the house. When dawn cast a pink shadow on the horizon he finally got up and went inside, no closer to a solution than he'd been before.

Nita stormed into the family room, feeling as if she were about an inch from her wits' end and slipping fast.

The men in this house were all acting like a bunch of fools and, damn it, it was time she did something about it.

She smacked the newspaper down on the coffee table across from her father's chair. Startled, he looked up from his game.

"What's the matter with you?"

She pointed at the paper. "You want to explain to me why there's no ad in this paper for a housekeeper when you assured me that you were going to take care of it."

He looked away, but not before she saw the guilt in his eyes. "Musta forgot."

Forgot my foot. "You haven't noticed the house is falling apart? Daddy, I am only one woman. I can't do it all. You, of all people, should know that."

"I'll start helpin' out then," he grumbled.

She doubted that. All he'd done since the hospital was sit on his duff and mope. Between him and Connor— who had grown even more withdrawn and cranky since their talk the other night—she was beginning to believe both men had developed some sort of weird, male PMS.

And even if her daddy did get off his behind and lend a hand, which at this point didn't look promising, he was limited as to what he could do in a cast.

It was time she put her foot down.

"That's not good enough," she told him. "We have to hire someone."

"It just… I can't do that."

"But we need a housekeeper!"

"It feels wrong to bring a new housekeeper in. This is Jane's house."

"*Jane's* house? I thought you built this house for Momma?"

If she'd been trying to push a button, she'd apparently hit the right one. He looked crestfallen. And for the first time since Jane left she realized he wasn't just being stubborn. He was genuinely hurt and lonely and confused.

"I never realized how much I would miss Jane," he said.

Nita knelt on the floor by his chair. "Then you have to tell her how you feel."

"When she comes back, I will."

"*Comes back?* Daddy, she isn't coming back."

He turned back toward the television. "She will, when she cools off, then I'll talk to her."

Nita groaned and let her head drop to the arm of the chair. So much for him not being stubborn. And here she'd actually felt sorry for him. The man obviously knew nothing about the inner workings of the female mind. If he thought Jane was going to come crawling back to him, he was in for a surprise.

If Will wouldn't go after Jane, maybe Nita should. Maybe Jane would swallow her pride, come back and listen to what Nita's daddy had to say. Short of hog-tying her daddy, throwing him in the truck and taking him to Odessa against his will, she didn't see a solution to this.

Something had to be done.

She left her daddy sulking in front of the television and set out to find Connor. He'd been outside talking with Jimmy when she went inside with the paper, so she headed through the kitchen to the back door.

"Where do you think you're going?" Connor snapped from behind her.

She turned to find him standing in the mudroom

doorway, arms folded over his chest, face pinched with irritation.

"I was coming out to look for you," she said.

"Uh-huh. Sure you were."

She felt like smacking him upside the head. "What, you think I'm lying?"

"Wouldn't be the first time you tried to sneak away from me."

"I thought you were still outside, and I was coming to talk to you."

The look of accusation didn't waver, nor did his aggravated tone. "Whatever you say."

No doubt about it, male PMS. That's what she got for trying to help him the other night. Silly her, she'd thought he would be grateful, or at least start acting human. And she was going to spend an hour in the car with him driving to Odessa?

Don't think so.

If he was so determined to believe the worst, that's exactly what she would give him. When the opportunity presented itself.

She folded her arms over her chest, imitating his stubborn stance. "Well, Mr. Crabby Pants, if you'd like, you could put a collar and a leash on me. Or how about an electronic ankle tether? Then you would always know where I am."

Connor tried to work up the will to be angry at her, since that seemed to be what she was aiming for, but all he felt was tired and frustrated. He knew he'd been difficult the past couple of days, and he had no right to take it out on her. Kind of like shooting the messenger considering, thanks to her, he'd come to realize his life was total crap.

Well, not *total* crap. He had the Cattleman's Club, and a brother who, despite Connor's persistent bad attitude and bitterness, still loved him and wanted what was best for him. And he had Nita—a woman he was falling hard for. But she didn't want a relationship. She only wanted him for sex.

Great.

"I'm going outside to work," Nita told him. "Is that okay with you?"

Since he didn't figure she expected a reply, he didn't bother to give her one. He just followed her as she stormed out the back door, contemplating the irony of the situation. Because of her, he could finally see the mistake he'd made living his life to please everyone else, and he was ready to take something for himself. Yet, once again, happiness evaded him. He'd spent the better part of his life distancing himself from women, taking only what he wanted and never letting anyone too close. Now the tables had turned on him. Apparently he was getting his just deserts. And he couldn't deny he deserved it.

That didn't make it any easier though.

Nita disappeared into the stable and Connor leaned against the fence. He closed his eyes and turned his face up into the sun, absorbing its heat, contemplating his next move. The one thing he knew he had to do, the thing that would be the most difficult, would be telling his father he was leaving the engineering firm permanently. He wasn't sure how the old man would take it. He was used to Connor doing what was expected of him. There would be shouting and disappointment. Nothing Connor hadn't heard before, and nothing he couldn't handle.

Short of that, he wasn't sure what he planned to do with the rest of his life. But of one thing he was certain, he wouldn't be making a decision until he was damned sure he was doing it for himself.

He heard a loud curse from the stable and snapped to attention. That was definitely Nita, and something was wrong, he could hear it in her voice. He broke into a run and reached the stable door just as she was limping out, her face a pale mask of pain.

He caught her under one arm. "What happened."

"Adonis got spooked and stomped on my foot." She cringed. "Damn it all, that smarts."

"Let me take a look." He knelt down beside her and gently pulled on her boot.

She gasped and yanked her foot away. "Hurts too much."

"Can you walk at all?"

She tried to put weight on her foot and shrieked in pain. She shook her head.

"Sounds like it's broken. I'd better get you to the hospital."

"I can't have a broken foot," she wailed. "Who's going to run the farm?"

"Until you're back on your feet, I will." The words came out before he had a chance to think it through, but he realized, he didn't mind. And not because it was the right thing to do. He really enjoyed working the farm. Working with the horses. It was…fun.

"I can't ask you to do that," Nita said.

"You didn't ask me. Let's worry about it after we get you taken care of." Connor lifted her as though she weighed nothing at all and Nita wrapped her arms around his neck, burying her face in his shoulder as he carried her to his car.

"I'm sorry," she said, feeling only slightly guilty as his strong arms cradled her. He was being a lot sweeter about this than she'd anticipated. It would be a whole lot easier if he was annoyed with her. If he didn't smell so good.

"No need to apologize." He pulled his keys from his jeans pocket and unlocked the car door, then he opened it and sat her gently on the seat. When she was settled in, he jogged around and climbed in, starting the car.

"Wait!" she said. "My insurance card. I have to have it."

"Tell me where it is and I'll go grab it."

"Upstairs in my room, on my dresser. And we have to tell Daddy what happened. He'll be worried."

"I'll be right back."

Nita waited until Connor had entered the house, then she tore the keys from the ignition, flung the car door open and ran like the devil was after her to the truck. She tossed Connor's keys on the front seat and yanked hers from her pocket, then she hopped in, shoved the key in the ignition and gunned the engine. She'd just like to see him catch her this time.

Spraying gravel and dust, she took off, glancing in the rearview mirror just in time to see Connor emerge from the house. She couldn't see his face, but she knew he had to be furious.

Somebody give the girl an Academy Award because she'd sure fooled him. She hoped he was kicking himself for falling for her phony broken foot routine.

She took a sharp right onto the road and floored it,

buried the needle at seventy, giving herself a nice long head start. That's what he got for thinking he could out-smart her. By the time he found Jimmy, got the keys for the other truck then figured out where she was headed, she would be halfway to Odessa.

Grinning to herself, she hummed along to the song playing on the radio. She reached the first in a series of curves in the road and hit the brake, but the pedal felt soft, as though she'd lowered her foot into a damp sponge.

Huh, that was weird.

She let up and tried again, and this time her foot went straight to the floor. Even worse, the truck didn't appear to be slowing down.

Oh, this was not good.

She stomped harder on the brake and *nothing* happened. The truck didn't stop.

Her heart stalled in her chest.

"Stay calm," she told herself, gripping the wheel, fighting to keep the truck on the road through the curve. When she was back on straight even road, she tried the brake again, sure it was some temporary malfunction, and still nothing. Fear gripped her when she realized she really had no brakes. She had no way to stop, and in an-other few miles she would run out of road. She would either have to turn right, or left, which would be virtu-ally impossible at this speed. She had to try to slow down. She had to calm down and think.

The ignition! She fumbled for the key, but at the last second hesitated. With the car off, would she lose steer-ing? If she couldn't stop *or* steer she'd really be in trou-ble. Instead, she grabbed the gearshift and popped it into neutral. The truck instantly began to slow, but at this rate she still wouldn't stop soon enough. Fences spanned either side of the road so running off into a field and coasting to a stop wouldn't work.

She knew that whatever she did, she could not let herself panic.

On her belt, her phone started ringing. Probably Connor, calling to chew her a new one. She wasn't exactly in the mood to chat so she let it go to voice mail. Less than a minute later, as she was scrambling to decided what to do next, it rang again.

She tore it from the case and flipped it open, telling him, "Now's *really* not a good time."

"Put the truck in neutral."

It *was* Connor. What the—? "How did you know—?"

"Just do it. *Now*."

"I did already. Where are you?"

"Behind you. Now, pull on the parking brake."

She looked in the rearview mirror, stunned to see Connor's car. How the heck did he—

"Nita! Listen to me. *You are running out of road.*"

She looked out the windshield and could see the intersection where she would have to turn looming ahead. At the speed she was going she would flip the truck. If she went straight, through the fence, she would mow down a couple of grazing horses. Definitely not an option.

"Use the parking brake. You're going to have to pull hard, and *don't* let go."

She dropped the phone on the seat and grabbed the lever for the brake, pulling with all her strength. The truck began to slow in short, jerky spurts. She saw Connor zip past her, then pull in front of the truck.

Was he *nuts?* She was going to run right into him!

Nita pulled harder on the brake, until her arm began to tremble. In front of her Connor gradually slowed until she felt her bumper tap the back of his car, then he applied his own brakes. She realized, he was helping her stop. She watched the needle on the speedometer gradually fall. It seemed to happen in slow motion, but they finally rolled to a complete stop about a hundred feet from the intersection.

Talk about cutting it close.

With a trembling hand, she put the truck in Park and killed the engine. The reality of what just happened hit her like a horse kick to the belly. She leaned back against the headrest and tried to tame her wildly pounding heart.

Connor's car door flew open and he got out. The second she saw him she knew he was furious. Radical plastic surgery couldn't make the lines in his face any tauter. She could just imagine the lecture she was going to get from this one. Not that she didn't deserve it. She'd been dumb with a capital *D*.

He stalked to the truck and yanked the door open. She braced herself for the explosion, for the reaming she knew was coming. The one she'd more than earned. Instead Connor just looked at her for a second, then he grabbed her and pulled her from the seat and straight into his arms.

Ten

When her boots hit the road Nita's legs buckled underneath her but Connor caught her and lifted her. She wrapped her legs around his waist, clinging to him, and he hugged her tight against his chest. He carried her away from the truck and sat on the hood of his car with her still wrapped around him. Now that it was over, and she was safe, her entire body began to tremble and she felt dizzy and fuzzy-headed, as if she might pass out.

Adrenaline.

This had happened once before when she'd been thrown by a stallion and almost trampled. Afterward she'd felt weak and shaky. But not like this.

Connor stroked her back, her hair. "Are you okay?"

She nodded against his shoulder.

"Don't you ever, *ever* pull a stunt like that again, you hear me?" Intermingled with the anger in his voice, she could swear she heard fear. Which meant he still cared about her, despite how he'd been acting lately. Nothing like a near-death experience to make someone admit he liked you.

Well, hell, if she'd known this was all it would take, she'd have staged her near-death weeks ago.

She heard another vehicle approaching, knew from the squeal of the brakes as it slid to a stop that it was the other farm truck. For the first time in her life she didn't care what the boys would think seeing her this way. She didn't care about being in control. She didn't even care if she looked weak. She just wanted Connor to hold her.

She heard doors open and slam shut, then Jimmy's voice. "She okay?"

"Yeah," Connor said. "Just scared."

"I called the sheriff like you asked. He's on his way."

"Thanks, Jimmy. Make sure the boys know not to touch anything."

"Will do. If you don't need us here, I'm gonna get back. Her daddy is worried something fierce. I want to let him know she's okay."

"We're going to wait here for the sheriff," Connor said, still rubbing her back in slow, soothing circles.

She heard the scuffle of boots, then the truck doors opened and closed. The engine roared to life and she heard them pull away in the opposite direction.

"You okay now?" Connor asked.

"I'm okay," she said, but he didn't let go, didn't even loosen his grip on her.

"How did you know about the brakes?"

"There was brake fluid all over the driveway where the truck was sitting."

"But your car? I took your keys."

"I keep a spare in my wallet."

She gave a shaky laugh. "Not much of an escape artist, am I?"

And thank God for that. Connor didn't even want to consider what might have happened had he not gotten to her in time. He never would have forgiven himself if she'd been hurt.

He closed his eyes and breathed in her scent, felt her warm, moist breath caressing the side of his neck. He was so relieved, so grateful she was safe, he felt weak-kneed. And he wanted to get his hands on whoever had done this. He wanted to rip them to pieces.

"Did I hurt your car?" she asked.

"I don't give a damn about the car." He'd have happily totaled it if it meant she was okay.

"I really screwed up." Her voice sounded stronger now and she'd stopped trembling.

"Yep."

"I thought you would be mad at me."

He had been. As soon as his car came to a stop his mind had gone into overload thinking of a million different ways he could punish her for being so foolish, for scaring the holy hell out of him. He'd yanked open the truck door, ready to lay into her.

Until he'd seen her face.

He'd seen corpses with more color. He knew right then, if there was a lesson to be learned, she'd learned it, and all the yelling and cursing he could do wouldn't compare to the scare she'd just had. All she'd needed was someone to hold her.

When he'd pulled her out of the truck and she'd clung

to him, her arms so tight around his neck he could barely breathe, her legs clamped like a vise around his waist, whatever was left of his anger dissolved into the cool, dusty air. To see her so scared, so vulnerable, made him sick in his soul.

He tried to imagine what would have happened if he hadn't gotten to her in time, if she'd been hurt, and his chest clenched so tightly he could hardly draw a breath. He didn't know what happened to him in those minutes between the time that he saw the brake fluid on the driveway, and the point when he'd opened the truck door, but he felt irrevocably changed.

All he knew, the only thing he was *certain* of, was now that he had her in his arms, he didn't ever want to let go.

"I'm so sorry," she said softly and he had to swallow the lump forming in his throat.

"Not as sorry as I would be if I'd let something happen to you." He stroked her back, tunneled his fingers through her hair, let himself really feel her—the long length of her body curled around him, the heat of her skin radiating through her shirt, the softness of her breasts against his chest. Her pulse vibrated through him like an electric charge, jump-starting the heart that had lain dormant inside him for so long. He could feel his body waking to her touch, his resolve weakening, and he let it happen. He'd been fighting so long and hard, he was too tired to do it another second. It was a relief to finally let go. To give in.

Nita leaned back to look at him, so young and vulnerable. She reached up and touched his face, smoothed an unsteady hand across his cheek, a look of longing in her eyes.

He lost it.

For once in his life, he was going to take what *he* wanted.

He cupped her face in his hands, brushed his lips across hers, and the sensation traveled through him like a wrecking ball, knocking down the invisible barrier he'd kept around his emotions. For the first time since he couldn't remember when, he was letting himself feel something other than the heavy hand of responsibility or that tedious sense of regret he'd grown so tired of. And the anger, the rage that gripped him at the slightest provocation—it was gone.

With Nita in his arms, he felt excited and peaceful and restless all at once. Her mouth was hot and sweet as their breath mingled. Tongues touched. So lightly, as if they wanted to linger in that perfect moment. And it *was* perfect, he realized. Nothing had ever felt so right to him.

He had to touch her, had to have his hands on her body.

He pulled her shirt from the waist of her jeans and slid his hands up her back, over her bare skin. She moaned softly, kissing him deeper, showing him once again she wasn't afraid to take what she wanted. He slipped his hands around to cup her breasts and her legs tightened about his waist, her body riding intimately against him. He was the one who groaned this time. He wrapped his hands around her rear end, pulled her even more firmly against him. He could feel himself losing control, the kiss going from demanding to reckless, but he didn't care. He wanted to touch every inch of her, taste her skin. He wanted it hot and rough and sweaty. He wanted whatever she was willing to give him. Which he was guessing would be pretty much anything.

In the distance he heard an approaching car. Nita pulled away and they both turned to see the sheriff's SUV sailing toward them, lights flashing.

They swore simultaneously.

"Can we get rid of him?" she asked breathlessly.

Connor sighed and pressed his forehead to hers. "He's going to have to question you."

She looked at him and whatever fear had been there before was long gone. "If you could feel how wet I am right now, I'll bet you would find a way."

That mouth of hers never ceased to amaze him. And fascinate him. "We'll pick this up later."

"You can bet on it, cowboy. I don't care if the house catches fire. We are gonna get naked tonight and I'm going to show you everything you've been missing."

Gavin snapped his phone shut then turned to Nita, Connor and her father, all sitting in the family room, waiting for what Connor was sure would be bad news.

"There's no doubt about it," Gavin told them. "The line was cut."

Connor shook his head. "Whoever did this has gone too far. Nita could have been killed. This was attempted murder."

"And the sheriff's office is going to give it top priority," Gavin said, then he flashed Nita a stern look. "But you need to be more careful. Don't go anywhere without Connor."

Though Connor would have expected an argument from her, she was silent. In fact, she'd been quiet all afternoon and into the evening, answering only the questions she was asked, saying nothing more. Gavin had interviewed Nita, Connor and every member of the staff. They'd determined the line had to have been cut sometime the night before, but no one had seen or heard a thing.

"Have you folks ever thought about getting a watchdog?" Gavin asked. "It could deter someone from trespassing."

"Daddy and I are both allergic," Nita said.

"Well, I'll make sure my deputy takes a few passes by the farm every night, but that's about the best I can do for now. We just don't have the manpower to watch all the property."

"Whatever you can do to help," Will said. "I'm just glad you're finally taking this feud seriously."

"Will, you have to remember that, until we have evidence to the contrary, this has nothing to do with the feud. Throwing accusations around will only make things worse." Gavin turned to Connor. "If anything comes up or if I have more questions, I'll be in touch."

"I'll walk you out," Connor said. He led Gavin through the house to the door.

When they were on the porch Gavin asked, "She realizes how serious this is now?"

"She knows. She had a hell of a scare today."

"Yeah, she looked pretty scared when I pulled up. I thought I was going to have to arrest you both for public indecency."

For the first time in his life he was taking something *he* really wanted, he'd be damned if he was going to apologize to anyone for it. "You got a problem with that?" he snapped.

Gavin laughed and held both hands up. "No problem

at all, Connor. I think Nita is a fine woman. You're a lucky man."

Didn't he know it. "Call me if you get any new information. I want you to nail whoever did this."

"Don't worry, we'll find him."

Gavin left and Connor went inside, locking the door behind him, wishing once again that they had a security system. When Clint had told Nita how much it would cost, she'd said absolutely not and wouldn't even discuss it. Maybe now she would reconsider.

He locked the kitchen door, then walked back to the family room, found Nita and her father sitting together on the couch. His arm was around her and her head was resting on his shoulder. Connor couldn't help feeling a stab of envy. Will showed Nita more love and affection than Connor's parents ever had combined. He'd always been taught to hide his feelings, that speaking his mind only got him a whack with the belt. The only way he knew how to please his father, the only way he had known how to measure up, was to follow in the old man's footsteps. To be everything his father expected. And in spite of it all, Connor had never gotten the approval he'd longed for. Never felt good enough.

The further he stepped back and really examined his life, the more bitter he felt. But bitterness had gotten him where he was now. If he was ever going to be happy, he needed to let it go.

"House is all locked up," he said.

Nita yawned long and deep. "I know it's early yet, but I'm exhausted. I think I'm just going to head up to bed."

"Go ahead," her father said, patting her arm. "Get some sleep. You'll feel better in the morning."

"Are you going to need help getting to bed?" Nita asked.

"No sweetheart, I can get by just fine."

"'Night, Daddy." She kissed her father good-night then got up from the couch. As she walked past Connor, she flashed him a lingering look. "'Night Connor."

She really did look tired and she'd been through hell today, still, Connor couldn't help feeling a healthy dose of disappointment. All afternoon he'd been looking forward to this evening, to see if he could get her as wet as she'd claimed to be earlier. But she'd had a long, trying day and it had probably caught up with her.

Maybe tomorrow.

"I guess I'll head up to bed, too," Connor told Will. "I have some reading to catch up on."

"Thank you for takin' care of my girl."

"No need to thank me," Connor said.

"Yes, there is. You see this," he said, raking a hand through his short, salt-and-pepper hair. "Used to be jet-black, just like Nita's. I've got one gray hair for every stunt that girl ever pulled, every scare she's ever given me, and as you can see there have been quite a few."

Connor grinned. "Yes, sir."

"She also has a heart of gold. I know she's been trying to shelter me from the truth, but I looked at the books the other day. I know how bad things are, and I know that you've been working without pay because of it."

The last thing he needed was for Nita's father to think he had ulterior motives. "We worked out a deal. Nita's been teaching me the business in exchange for my help."

"Despite being a little wild at times, Nita has a soft side. And though you would never know it, she bruises easily, even if she doesn't let it show. Any man who dared hurt her would have to deal with me."

Connor wasn't sure if that was a general threat, or aimed at him in particular. "Only after they got through me," he said.

Will just looked at him for a minute, then nodded. "I believe you. And I want you to know I appreciate all you've done for us these past couple weeks. You're part of the family now, and you'll always have a place here with us, understand?"

Connor was so choked with unexpected emotion, he could only nod.

Will nodded back, then picked up the controller and switched the television on. "See you in the morning."

"G'night."

Leaving Will alone in the family room, Connor headed up the stairs, vowing that, if he ever had a family, he would raise his children the way Will had. They would always feel loved and appreciated for who they were.

A wife and family.

For the first time in his life he realized he wanted that. He wanted those things with Nita.

And she didn't want them with anyone, not even him.

He stepped into his room, but before he could even switch the lights on, a pair of arms circled him from behind.

"Ready to play, cowboy?"

Connor turned and Nita rose up on her toes to kiss him. She loved the taste of his mouth, the softness of his tongue, the brush of his whiskers against her chin.

Most men kissed too hard or too soft, or too sloppy. Connor, no matter how he did it, was always just right.

Their lips still locked, he pulled her into the room and shut the door. She tore his shirt from the waist of his jeans, desperate to get him naked, before something else happened to sidetrack them. She grabbed the two sides of his shirt and yanked.

Button's flew everywhere and bounced across the hardwood floor. She pushed the shirt off his shoulders and down his arms.

"You are a wild one," Connor muttered as she slid her hands up his bare chest, sank her teeth into his lower lip.

"Do mine now," she said, kissing her way to his ear, sucking his lobe into her mouth. She wouldn't be happy until she licked and sucked every bit of him. "Rip it off me."

Connor slipped his fingers into the gaps between the buttons of her shirt, lightly stroking the skin beneath. She liked foreplay, but she was so ready for him she felt like she would burst into flames if he didn't take her soon.

"Do it," she said, and still he only teased.

"You in some kind of hurry?" he asked, and she could hear amusement in his voice.

"In fact I am. If we don't get this show on the road something is bound to happen that will stop us again. A meteor could hit the house or World War Three could break out."

His fingers brushed the skin just below her bra and she shivered. "I thought you were exhausted."

"Do I look exhausted to you?"

"I guess not." With one quick yank he ripped the shirt open and a second round of buttons went airborne.

He pushed the shirt off her, then instead of reaching back to undo her bra, he gave that a yank too. Nita gasped as the garment ripped clear in half. It made her so hot she felt dizzy.

He cupped his warm hands over her breasts. "Better?"

"Oh, yes." She sighed and closed her eyes. She liked a man who took charge every now and then. It wasn't often she found one who could keep up with her. One that wasn't intimidated by her aggressive nature.

"I want to see you," he said. He backed toward the bed, pulling her along with him, and switched on the lamp.

Warm light poured over him and she took in the sight of all his thick, bulky muscle. The man did have a body to die for, and she was going to touch it all.

"You're beautiful," he said, his eyes roaming over her as if the sight of her body amazed him.

Poor guy. He obviously didn't get out much if he thought she was beautiful. Not that she was ugly. She was always okay with her body. It didn't seem to turn anyone off, even though she didn't have much in the way of a figure. Small breasts, no hips to speak of— nothing special. She did have a few special skills that she planned to use on him as soon as she got the rest of his clothes off. And she could see from the generous ridge in the front of his jeans, she was going to have a lot to play with.

She unbuttoned his pants and was working on the zipper when Connor caught her wrist in his hand.

"Nita wait. Not yet."

She closed her eyes and sighed. *Good lord, here we go again.*

Eleven

"Wait for what?" Nita asked Connor.

"There's something I need to say to you."

Was he kidding? They'd come this far and now he wanted to stop and *talk?* It just wasn't normal.

She pulled her hand free and slid it up his chest. "Would you mind terribly if we talked later?"

He grabbed her hand and held it. "In fact I would mind."

The man was impossible! She blew out a long frustrated breath. "Okay, what do you need to say?"

"I need you to know that this isn't just sex to me. Today, when I thought about losing you…" He shook his head, as though he couldn't bear to say the words.

"I'm not lost," she told him.

"Nita—"

She pressed her fingers over his mouth. "No more

talking tonight, okay? Let's just concentrate on making each other feel good."

It wasn't that she didn't like to talk. She simply was afraid of what he might say. They'd both had a scare and their emotions were running high. High enough to make him say things he didn't really mean. Things she didn't ever want to hear from a man. Things that would tempt her to give more of herself than was wise.

He cradled her face in his hands and kissed her. A slow, sweet kiss packed with more raw emotion than she knew what to do with. More emotion than she could take right now. Despite what he thought, this was sex and nothing more. It's all it could ever be. She couldn't let herself fall in love with him.

She backed away and unfastened her jeans, pushing them down along with her panties. His eyes raked over her, so filled with heat she was afraid her skin might catch fire.

Now, this was more like it.

Connor shoved his pants down and kicked them out of the way. For a minute they just looked, devouring each other with their eyes. The lower half of him was just as amazing as the top. She couldn't wait to taste and touch all of it.

He reached for her but she backed away.

"Uh-uh. Lay down."

"What are you going to do?" He didn't sound worried, just inquisitive.

She ran her tongue across her bottom lip. "Things you've only dreamed about."

He sat on the edge of the mattress, scooted back and stretched out in all his glory with his hands folded under his head on the pillow. Not bashful, was he? "This what you wanted?"

"Perfect." Nita knelt at the foot of the bed and crawled up between his legs. Starting at his ankles, she ran her hands up, through the crisp dark hair. She felt the muscle flex under her palms and his eyes grew heavy with lust.

She lowered her head and ran her tongue up the entire length of his erection.

Connor groaned and gripped the bottom edge of the headboard. Nita sure didn't waste any time getting to the good stuff. And he didn't doubt it would only get better.

For a while she only teased him, using her tongue in ways he hadn't even known were possible. He lay there in ecstasy wondering where she'd learned to do this, how many men had come before him, then realized he didn't care. He was here now. That was all that mattered.

When he didn't think he could take much more of her exploring, she looked up to make sure he was watching and took him deep in her mouth. It was so damned erotic he just about lost it. It wasn't the first time a woman had gone down on him but he couldn't remember it feeling this good. He couldn't remember feeling much of anything at all. He'd never let himself.

Now he couldn't stop feeling. The wet heat of her mouth, the soft scrape of her teeth on his skin, her hair slipping like silk across his thighs. Her palms were rough from handling the horses, but instead of it being a turn-off, it only excited him more. Everything about her excited him. Too much. His heart pounded, blood pulsed as desire took hold and wouldn't let go. He wanted it to last but it felt so damned good. He was almost there…

About half a second before he reached the point of no return, she gave him one more long, wet lick, then stopped. He groaned with both disappointment and relief.

She started kissing a path up his belly, slid herself over his body, touching and tasting everything along the way, until she was straddling him. For the rest of his life he would never forget the way she looked sitting there, long and lean and beautiful. He thought about what she'd said, about looking like a boy and nearly laughed out loud.

"See how wet you make me?" She rocked herself intimately against him, so hot and slippery. He groaned and dug his fingers into her hips. He didn't want to rush this, but he was so turned on he couldn't see straight.

"Connor, I need you inside me. I can't wait any longer."

"Do I need my wallet?"

"I'm on the pill," she said. "Is that okay?"

"Works for me." He watched as, eyes closed, head thrown back, she lowered herself over him, took him deep inside of her. She was so hot and tight he was sure he'd died and gone to heaven. Nothing should ever feel this good, this perfect.

For several seconds she sat motionless, as if savoring the moment, then she began to move. If he'd expected slow and sweet, he could see right away that wasn't going to happen. She rode him hard and fast, whispering sexy words in a voice husky with desire. All too soon he began to lose himself in the exquisite sensations, but instead of trying to lock it down as he normally would, wring all the feeling, all the emotion from the act, he let go. He let himself feel it all—physically and emotionally. It came from everywhere and nowhere, and was more intense than anything he'd ever felt before. And when he knew he was ready to tumble over the edge, his body didn't let go. The world around him became a blur as sensation like he'd never felt overwhelmed him. It drove him higher and higher, until it was almost too much to take.

Then Nita cried out and her body clamped hard around him and he lost it. Orgasm for him had always been swift and simple—a release of pent-up energy. What was happening to him now… It was as if every emotion he'd never let himself feel came crashing down around him all at once. It was almost too much to bear. Too painfully intense. He was still riding it out when Nita collapsed breathlessly in his arms.

That's when he knew what he'd told her was true. This wasn't just sex to him. He loved her. She was what he wanted, for the rest of his life, and he would do whatever it took to keep her.

Nita lay sprawled across Connor's chest, listening to his heart pound against her ear, feeling the deep rise and fall as he breathed.

Normally she didn't do the whole afterglow routine. It was too personal, too easy to drop her defenses and let those warm, fuzzy feelings mess with her head. But for some reason, she couldn't seem to make herself get out of his bed. She didn't *want* to.

She had known sex with him would be good, but they'd blown right past good the second he'd ripped her bra off. From there she couldn't even put into words what she'd felt because there were really no words to describe it. He was definitely in a class all by himself.

For a fleeting moment she'd worried that, given his age, she might be too much for him to handle, but he'd had the stamina of men half his age—and then some. And while she'd expected him to be as reserved in bed as he had been in personality, he'd quickly proved her wrong. He'd arranged her in so many different positions—some downright scandalous—that by the time they were finished she'd felt like a human pretzel. Who would have guessed a man as reserved and quiet as Connor would have such an adventurous streak in bed?

Connor stroked her back with a large, warm hand—down her spine, over the curve of her behind and back up again. "Is it safe to talk now?"

"What do you mean?"

"You told me earlier, no more talking tonight. But I figured since it's 1:00 a.m., it's technically tomorrow."

"We have been talking," she said. There was no way he could accuse her of being quiet during sex.

"By talking, I mean having a conversation, not, 'Do it harder, Connor,' or 'Faster, Connor.'"

She laughed and pinched him playfully. "Yeah, okay. What do you want to talk about?"

"I don't know. What do you usually talk about after sex?"

"I don't. Unlike most women, I'm the first one off the bed and out the door."

"Why is that?"

She shrugged. "Never seemed much point in hanging around. You do and a man starts to get the wrong idea."

"But you're here now."

"You wore me out. I'm too tired to move." It wasn't a complete lie, and it was easier than the truth. Hell, even she didn't know why she was still lying there. It had to be temporary insanity.

"Have there been many before me?"

She could swear she heard a sour note in his voice. She got up on her elbow and peered at him though the dark. "You jealous, Connor?"

If he was, his face didn't reveal a thing. "Just curious."

"Well, it's less than you'd probably think. Three not including you." She propped her chin on his chest. "How about you?"

"More than three."

Meaning he wasn't going to tell her. That was okay, because if it was an astronomical number, like two hundred, she didn't even want to know. "How old were you when you lost your virginity?" she asked instead.

"We were both seventeen."

She tried to imagine Connor at seventeen, before life had hardened his face, what a heartbreaker he must have been. The girls must have flocked to him. "I'll bet you drove the poor girl wild," she said.

He chuckled. "I wish. I was so nervous I could barely get the condom on and I lasted all of about ten seconds. I doubt it was a memorable experience. How about you, when was your first time?"

"I was nineteen."

He looked surprised. "I would have guessed younger."

"Jane had hammered into me for years that I should save myself for marriage. Not that I didn't do my fair share of fooling around."

He stroked a big hand up her arm, across her shoulder. "Your curious nature?"

"Exactly. But I got to thinking that maybe I didn't ever want to get married. So, it was either die a virgin, or have some harmless fun."

"Makes sense I guess."

"And it's not like I went to a bar and picked some stranger out of the crowd. I was particular when it came to choosing the right man. A couple of months went by and I thought maybe I would never find him, then Jimmy hired a new hand and the second I saw him, I knew he would be the one. He was twenty-nine."

Connor raised an eyebrow. "Twenty-nine, huh?"

She grinned. "What can I say, I've got a thing for older men. We got serious for a while. I even thought I loved him."

"What happened?"

"He inherited his granddaddy's ranch in Montana. He wanted me to marry him and move there."

"I take it you said no."

"At first I thought about going, even though I would miss Daddy something fierce. We talked about it, and he encouraged me to follow my heart. Ranching sounded like fun and I figured I could start up a horse training business. Until this man made it clear that he would run the ranch and *I* would cook and clean and become a baby machine. He wanted six kids! Can you believe that?"

"You don't want kids?"

"Maybe one or two. But *six?* I said no way, I wasn't going to be anybody's domestic slave."

"Good thing," Connor said. "One week of your cooking and he'd have sent you straight back to Texas."

Some women might have been offended by his re-mark. She only laughed. "I'm just not cut out for do-mestic life. Even though people in town don't think that's right. They think being raised without a mother messed me up somehow."

"What do you think?"

"I don't care what they think. I was born this way and if they don't like it they can all go to hell. The more they push me, I push back twice as hard. I'm sure you've heard things."

"Yeah," he admitted. "I've heard a thing or two."

"How about you?" she asked. "Ever been married?"

"Nope."

"Ever come close?"

"Never."

"Have you ever been in love?"

"I never let myself get that close to a woman," he said, reaching up to stroke her cheek. "This is different."

A tangle of emotions she didn't want to feel wrapped themselves around her heart and squeezed. She didn't even want to know what he'd meant by that.

She laid her head on his chest and closed her eyes, afraid of what she might see if she dared look at him again. Somehow the conversation had gone from casu-ally playful to solemn and profound and she just couldn't deal with it right now. "It's late, I should go to bed."

"I thought you were too tired to move."

"I've had time to recover."

His hand wandered down to stroke her behind. "Guess I'll just have to wear you out again."

"I think it's better if I just go." She made a move to leave and his arms went around her, holding her close to him.

"Don't go, Nita."

There was world of feeling packed into those three little words. She wanted to hate it, wanted to run and hide, but then he started kissing her, started touching her, and all she could do was melt.

One night, she decided as he rolled her over, started kissing his way down under the covers. She'd give him one full night.

He parted her legs, touched her with his mouth and she groaned with pleasure.

One night together, then things were going to change.

Nita endorsed the checks that had arrived in the mail that afternoon and set them in the top drawer, ready for her weekly trip to the bank. She swallowed the knot of anxiety that had lodged itself in her throat and tried to convince herself things would be okay—she could hold it together. With so much of their business lost, compounded by the vet bills from the poisoned feed, things were even worse than she'd thought. The worst they'd ever been.

She hoped the Devlins were happy. They'd been trying for years to get their hands on the land and this time they just might have succeeded. A few more months of this and she and her daddy might have to sell.

The phone rang, but when she looked at the caller ID she didn't recognize the number. "Windcroft's, Nita speaking."

"Nita, honey, it's Jane."

"Jane!" Nita felt a gush of relief. "It's so good to hear your voice. Please tell me you've decided to come back."

There was a pause, then Jane said, "I'm sorry, but I'm

not coming back. I heard what happened with the truck and I was calling to see that you're all right."

Nita's disappointment felt like a swift jab to her chest. She wished her father would stop being such a pain and just ask Jane to come home. *Beg* her, if that's what it took. "I'm okay," Nita said. "Just had a bit of a scare."

"Is Connor still there with you?"

She glanced through the open office door to the bench where Connor sat, his nose buried in Jane's book. "Yep. My own personal G.I. Joe. He's sitting out in the foyer as we speak, guarding the office door."

"I'm glad. I don't know what I'd do if anything happened to you or…" She trailed off, her voice sad.

"Jane, please come home. We miss you. Daddy has been downright miserable with you gone. Not to mention the house is falling apart and he refuses to hire a new housekeeper. He's convinced you're coming back."

"That's exactly why I can't."

"I know he loves you. He's just so darned stubborn. I was on my way to come talk to you when the brakes went out."

"Well, I could have saved you the trip. I couldn't live with myself if I went crawling back to him. I have to salvage what little dignity I have left and move on."

Nita could hear that she was close to tears. She hadn't realized until that moment just how deeply Jane had been hurt.

"Nita, I have to go."

"Jane, he'll come around."

She went on like Nita hadn't spoken. "Next time I'm in Royal maybe we can meet for lunch. Keep in touch."

"Jane—" The line went dead. Nita sighed and hung up.

"She's not coming back?"

Nita looked up, saw Connor standing in the office doorway.

"Nope. Not till my daddy asks her, and he won't talk to her till she comes back."

"That could be a problem."

"I swear, they're the two most stubborn people in the world. But I'll figure something out. A way to get them together." She closed her laptop, got up and met him at the door. She slid her hands up his chest and he looped his arms around her waist. His body was so big and sturdy and strong. She loved that she could touch him this way whenever the mood struck her. Which was happening an awful lot the past couple of days. "I was thinking I'd better go get cleaned up for dinner."

Connor looked at his watch. "It's only four."

"I'm going to need a shower. You being my bodyguard and all, you'll have to be there to keep me safe."

A grin curled his mouth. "I will, huh?"

"And you know what happens when I get you naked." She pressed a kiss to his rough chin. "I just can't keep my hands to myself. So we may need a couple of hours."

"What if your father catches us? I feel like I'm disrespecting him."

She rubbed herself against him, felt his body responding to her. "He won't climb the stairs in his cast. He'll never know. And I'm just dying to know what you look like soapy and wet."

The grin widened and she knew she had him. "Meet me in the bathroom in five minutes."

Twelve

"How's your dinner, Daddy?"

"It's fine," her daddy said, because he would never say anything to hurt her feelings. But *fine,* came nowhere near to describing what she'd set in front of him.

Rather than do her best to make dinner edible tonight, and since it was Friday and the men had gone out for the evening, she'd done all she could to make it as unpalatable as humanly possibly—which for her was second nature. She'd found an old loaf of bread shoved to the very back of the bread box under some old hot dog buns. It was dry, mashed flat in places and moldy on the edges. The stew was from a can, which in itself was bad enough, but she hadn't heated it all the way through and it looked like chunky, congealed gravy sitting in the bowl.

It was all part of her new plan to get her daddy and Jane back together.

"Speaking of cooking, Jane called today."

Her daddy didn't even look up from his bowl. If nothing else, he huddled even lower over it. "Oh yeah."

"She wants me to bring her the book with all the family recipes in it."

He didn't respond.

"She needs it for her new job."

He was trying his best to look disinterested, but she saw some unidentifiable emotion flicker in his eyes. "Got a new job, huh?"

"That's what she said."

"Guess that's good. Gotta make a living."

"That's what I thought, too, until she told me the details. She went to see Lucas Devlin about a job. He hired her on the spot, no references or anything."

Her daddy's knuckles turned white as he gripped his spoon tighter and Connor flashed her a questioning look. He knew darn well Jane had said no such thing.

"She seemed pretty taken with him," Nita continued, pouring gasoline on the fire. "She kept going on about what a nice man he is, and how we've been wrong about him all these years. She can't wait to start working for him next week."

Her daddy's face turned so red she thought his head might explode, but he didn't say a word. Now for the really good stuff.

She shook her head in mock disgust. "The way she talked, you'd have thought she had a crush on him or something."

Will slammed his spoon down on the table and stood, grabbing his crutches.

"You didn't finish your dinner," Nita said.

"Lost my appetite," he grumbled and stormed out of the kitchen—as best as a person could storm with a broken leg. A minute later she heard his bedroom door slam.

Connor was shaking his head. "You are such a liar."

"Well, I had to do *something*," Nita said, feeling completely justified in her actions. They couldn't survive this way much longer.

He pushed his bowl away, his stew barely touched. "Is that what this whole awful meal was about? You're trying to make him miss her cooking? Because even you can do better than this."

"If he really truly loves her, no way in hell he'll let her hook up with a Devlin. It couldn't be any worse if I'd said she was shacking up with Satan himself."

"And how are you going to explain it when they figure out they've been duped?"

"I won't have to. They'll be so happy to be together, they won't care."

"You better hope you're right." He balled his napkin and tossed it in his bowl. "Let's clean up this mess and get out of here."

"Where are we going?"

"It's chili night at the Royal Diner," he said.

When they pulled up the driveway two hours later, stuffed from a meal of chili and biscuits, the house was dark and both trucks were gone.

The men had taken one, meaning her father must have taken the other.

"He knows he's not supposed to drive," Nita said, and for the first time that evening showed a hint of reservation, as though she was beginning to wonder if lying to her father was such a hot idea after all.

"What did you expect?" Connor asked her as they climbed out of the car. "You made it sound like she and Lucas Devlin were getting ready to elope."

"I figured he'd call her. I didn't know he'd drive all the way to Odessa." A slow smile curled her mouth and she walked around to his side. "You know what this means, don't you?"

"I'm afraid to ask."

"We have the entire farm to ourselves." She slid her hands up his chest. "Where do you want to do it first?"

Earlier that afternoon it had been the shower, the night before that he'd taken her up against the wall in the stable after the hands had retired for the evening. The woman was downright insatiable.

"How about right here on your car?" she asked, step-ping backward toward the hood, unfastening the buttons on her shirt.

"Outside?"

"It's dark. No one will see."

"With all the mischief going on here, you can't be too sure of that."

Her grin faded. "I never thought of that."

"How about inside the house?"

She thought about that for a minute, tracing her fin-ger along the edge of her bra. "On the kitchen table maybe?"

"And suppose your father comes home. What then?"

The grin reappeared. "It's always more fun if you think you might get caught."

For her maybe, but she wouldn't be the one staring

down the barrel of her father's shotgun if they were discovered. "How about a good old-fashioned bed?" he asked. "That would be a nice change."

"Oh, all right," she conceded. "But this time we get to use my bed. Later, when I'm alone, I want to smell you on my sheets."

She took his hand and led him inside, not bothering to turn any lights on. They were halfway up the darkened stairs when his cell phone rang. Connor checked the display and cursed. He'd hoped to put this off another week or two. He could let it go to voice mail and deal with it later, but the truth was, he'd put it off long enough.

"I have to take this," he told Nita, who was already half-undressed and on her way down the hall.

Though he couldn't see her face clearly, there was concern in her voice. "Is everything okay?"

"It's my father."

She didn't question him, just nodded and said, "I'll be waiting for you," then disappeared into her bedroom. Most women would have been irritated by the interruption. Of course, Nita had never been like most women.

Connor went into his own room and shut the door, knowing this wasn't going to be pretty, and answered, "Hello, Father."

"Lyle Edwards tells me you haven't been in the office for several weeks now. I'd like an explanation."

No, *hello, son, how's it been, it's good to talk to you.* It was just like his father to dispense with the pleasantries and get to the point. And to use that tired old disappointed tone he was famous for. Connor wondered if he'd ever really heard himself, if he realized how he sounded. Or if it wouldn't matter to him either way.

"I've been busy," he told his father. "Cattleman's Club business."

His father made a noise of disgust. "You and your brother and that damned fool club."

Like most people, his father didn't know the extent of the Cattleman's Club dealings, the people they'd helped, and Connor wasn't in any mood to explain it. He didn't feel the need to justify his life any longer.

"You have responsibilities to the firm," his father continued. "I want you back in the office Monday morning."

There was no easy way to say this, no way to soften the blow, so Connor decided to come right out and say it. "I'm resigning from the firm, effective today."

"You can't do that," his father said, as if his word was law, which for the past thirty-eight years, it had been. He was in for a terrible shock, because things had changed.

"I *can* do it, and I will," Connor said. "I'm not happy there."

His father didn't miss a beat. "Your happiness is not my concern. I have a business to run. I'm counting on you to take care of things for me."

And didn't that sum it all up? It didn't matter what Connor wanted. His father was driven only by his own selfish needs.

"I'm sorry, I really am, but I'm not going back." He was even more sorry that he hadn't done this years ago, when his father decided it would be best for his wayward, aimless son to join the army. Connor may not have been sure what he wanted to do with his life, but it was a decision he should have made for himself.

"What is it you think you want to do then?" his father asked, his voice dripping with sarcasm.

He thought of Nita in the other room waiting for him. Nita, who was everything he could possibly want for a future. "Maybe horse farming," he told his father.

"*Horse* farming? That sounds like a supreme waste of your skills."

"Maybe, but they're mine to waste if that's what I choose."

"This is nonsense. I know what's best for you. The firm is your legacy. You can't turn your back on it."

"I don't want it."

"First the military, now this? What's gotten into you?"

His father would never understand, never concede, so there was really no point trying to explain. Not when his future was waiting in the next bedroom for him. "I know I'm disappointing you, but I can't live my life according to your grand plan any longer. Say hello to Mother for me. I'll talk to you later." He disconnected, turned his phone off and snapped it back on his belt. Then he took a long, deep breath. Instead of feeling bad for failing to please his father, he felt…free. He should have done this years ago.

If only he'd known.

He walked down the hall to Nita's room and knocked softly before opening the door. She lay naked on top of her covers with only the silver light of the moon shining over her. He'd never seen anything so beautiful, never wanted anything or anyone the way he wanted her.

And he would get her, she just didn't know it yet.

"Do you want to talk about it?" she asked.

He walked to the bed, unbuttoning his shirt. "I told him I'm resigning from the firm."

"How did he take it?"

"He wasn't happy." He tossed his shirt on the floor and unfastened his jeans. "He'll get over it."

She rose up on her elbows, watching him undress. "You did the right thing."

"I know I did." He shed the rest of his clothes and climbed on the bed beside her. Nita wrapped her arms around his neck, pressed the entire length of her body against him and kissed him like there was no tomorrow. Just like her to always be in a rush. But tonight, he wanted to make it last. He was going to make love to her. And little did she know, now that she'd gotten him into her bed, she was going to have a hell of a time getting him back out again.

Nita rubbed herself against Connor, loving the way his body responded to her touch. The way his muscles flexed and his skin went from warm to hot. She loved the way he tasted when they kissed. But more than anything else, she loved to sit over him, watch his face as she took him inside of her, watch that look of complete abandon, knowing she made him feel that way. She was able to make this big, strong, quiet soldier lose his cool.

It was unbelievably arousing, and just plain fun.

"Roll over," she said, pushing on his chest. "I want to be on top."

He looked down at her through the dark. "Why?"

She pushed with all her strength, but the man weighed a ton. "Because I do. I like it better that way."

"I want to make love to you, Nita. And I want to do it slow this time."

"Sex, Connor. Not Love. And you know I like it hard and fast." She tried again to push him away, but he grabbed her wrists and pinned her arms above her head. Ugh! The man was impossible. "Let go of me."

His grip tightened. "Nope."

She hooked her legs over his hips and arched against him, knowing that drove him nuts, but he wasn't fazed.

"That isn't going to work," he said. "This time we're doing it my way."

"I won't enjoy it," she insisted.

"How do you know until you've tried?"

"I *have* tried. Slow just doesn't…*do it* for me."

"Do it?"

Jeez, did he need her to spell it out? "I mean, I can't come like that."

He didn't look deterred. "I'll bet I can make you come."

"No, you can't."

A grin curled his mouth. "See, now you've gone and made it a challenge. Now I have to do it, even if it takes all night."

She blew out a long-winded sigh. Then this was going to be one long, boring night. "If it means that much to you."

"It does." He kissed the side of her neck—soft, slow kisses designed to tease and tempt her. Which they didn't…at least, not too much. It didn't exactly feel awful, either. But they sure wouldn't have her screaming in ecstasy. Although she had to admit being pinned was just a little exciting, it would get old real fast.

He nibbled her earlobe, and an involuntary shiver jerked though her. That was pure luck, she decided. Her ears had always been sensitive, so it didn't really count. And as good as it felt, it would take a lot more than that to make her come. She didn't know what he was trying to prove, but this wasn't going to work.

She wiggled restlessly beneath him, so he would know this wasn't any fun. He didn't even seem to notice.

He moved to her throat next, licked her there, and her traitorous head fell back on its own accord. Okay, so that felt pretty good. The man did have a way with his mouth.

He brushed his lips lightly over hers.

All right, this was more like it. Kissing she could definitely do, but when she tried to deepen the kiss, he backed out of reach.

Oh, that was so not fair. If he was going to kiss her, he should just do it. Instead he moved to the opposite side of her throat, licked her there, nibbled her other ear. At the rate he was going, this *would* take all night.

She pushed up against his hands, let out a frustrated groan, but he didn't stop. He licked and nibbled his way lower, across one shoulder, following the path of her collarbone to the opposite side. Maybe if he would touch her breasts this wouldn't be so bad, but every time he got close, when she felt his breath warm her nipple and she arched up toward his mouth, he'd become preoccupied somewhere else.

She could feel her skin growing warmer, feel herself getting wetter. Which didn't mean much considering all he had to do to get her wet was look at her the right way. Right now she was more frustrated than aroused.

He went for her mouth again, brushing his lips softly against hers. She did love kissing him. She lay perfectly still, knowing that if she so much as breathed hard she would stop again. He nibbled her upper lip, then the lower one, teasing with his tongue. She couldn't stop herself from touching her tongue to his, and the second she did, he backed away.

She felt like screaming. Was he trying to ruin this for her, trying to make her miserable?

He wound up at her throat again somehow, and slowly licked his way down, between her breasts. Her nipples pulled into tight, aching points. He ignored them completely and kept going lower, down each of her ribs, kissing them, one after another. As he descended, he let go of her wrists and she wrapped her hands around his head, tunneled her fingers through his hair. He sank lower still, kissing her belly, teasing her navel with the tip of his tongue.

Keep goin', she wanted to tell him, a little farther. Instead he started up. She tried to push him down but he brushed her hands out of the way.

"Don't make me tie you up," he warned. Considering the devilish gleam in his eye, she wouldn't put it past him to do exactly that. She let go of his head and fisted her hands in the blankets instead. He was going to pay for this, for torturing her. She felt like a rubber band stretched too tight and ready to snap.

Without warning he ran his tongue across the rounded underside of her breast. She was so surprised she gasped and nearly vaulted off the bed.

He looked up at her and grinned. "That must have felt awful."

"You just startled me," she said, surprised by how husky her voice sounded. Yeah, maybe she was turned on, but if he thought this was going to do the trick, he was wrong. He was moving too darned slow.

He licked the opposite breast the same way and though she tried to hold it in, a moan slipped from her throat.

He looked up at her and grinned. "Startled you again, did I?"

Oh, he was so smug. He wouldn't be so cocky later when he realized what a waste this had been. He wouldn't be smiling then.

His mouth closed around her nipple, sucked hard. She cried out and rocked against him.

He lifted his head to look at her. "You want me to make love to you, Nita?"

She shook her head.

He settled himself between her thighs. With the slightest shift he would be inside her. "You sure about that?"

She looked him in the eye and, using blunt language, told him exactly what she did want.

Though he pretended to look shocked, she knew he loved it when she talked dirty. "Someone needs to wash out that mouth of yours," he told her.

"Already been done," she said breathlessly. "It didn't help."

He shifted his hips, rubbed against her. She couldn't stop herself from arching up, seeking him out. He was killing her. She was dying a slow, agonizing death.

"Nita, look at me," he said.

She opened her eyes, looked up at him. His eyes were deep blue wells of emotion, and as much as she wanted to look away, she couldn't make herself do it.

His eyes still pinned on hers, he slowly entered her. She clung to him, sank her nails into his back. When he'd filled her completely he stopped for what felt like an eternity, then eased out and slowly pushed forward again. She wanted to tell him harder, faster, but her voice wouldn't work. She couldn't even focus.

If he didn't do something soon she *was* going to die. Her body was on fire, screaming for release and he moved in the same slow, steady rhythm. Then he lowered his head and kissed her, his mouth hot and sweet, his tongue rubbing sensuously against her own. She wasn't sure how it happened but one second she was in agony, the next ecstasy, gripped by the most fierce, most erotic orgasm she'd ever had in her life. All she could do was lie there, paralyzed by pleasure. And just when she thought it was over, when she caught her breath and the world came back into focus, she opened her eyes, saw Connor tense with his own release, heard him cry out her name, and she flew apart all over again.

Thirteen

Connor was helping Nita and Jimmy unload supplies from the truck the following morning when he heard a vehicle and turned to see Jake's black SUV pulling up the driveway. It wasn't like him to drop by for no reason. No doubt he'd gotten a call from their father.

"It's my brother," he told Nita. "I should talk to him."

"Go ahead," she said. "We'll finish up here, then I'll get lunch started. What sounds good? Burned grilled cheese or canned stew?"

"Burgers at the Royal Diner," he said, laughing and darting out of the way when she tried to swat him.

"You think you're so funny," she grumbled, but she was grinning, too.

He headed to his brother's car. Jake climbed out, a

perplexed look on his face, and as Connor got closer, he began to shake his head. "Look at you."

Connor stopped and looked down at him self. "What about me?"

"I don't know," Jake said. "You look…different. Your hair is longer."

Connor dragged a hand through the hair that was about six weeks past its monthly trim. "Yeah, haven't had time to get it cut. I'm thinking I might grow it out."

"It's not just that. You look relaxed and…I don't know. I guess you look happy."

"I am happy," he said, and for the first time in his life really meant it.

"I imagine that has a lot to do with the call I got from Dad last night."

Connor grimaced. He should have known after he shut his phone off their father would have been through the roof, hopping mad, and he would need someone to take it out on. "Yeah, sorry about that. I should have called and warned you."

Jake leaned against the hood of his car. "So, you finally did it. You told him off."

Connor could swear he saw admiration in his brother's eyes. Which didn't make sense because Jake had never held back when it came to putting their father in his place. "Actually no, I didn't. I just told him I was resigning from the firm. I didn't stay on the phone long enough to hear him rant. Nothing he could say would change my mind, so I hung up and turned my phone off."

"Which would explain why he called me."

"I'm sorry if he gave you a hard time."

He shrugged. "You know me. Everything he says

pretty much rolls off my back. But that isn't the only reason I'm here. Gavin got some new information."

"About the feud?"

"About Jonathan Devlin's death. It seems that Malcolm Durmorr worked at the hospital as an orderly at the time that Jonathan was injected. He was later dismissed on the recommendation of a board member— Opal Devlin."

"Meaning he could have something against the Devlins, and a reason to keep the feud going?"

"It's a possibility. He's had his share of run-ins with the law. And he's been seen with Gretchen. She has a horse here, doesn't she?"

Connor nodded. "Yeah, Nita said she doesn't ride it, though. She's only been here a couple of times to see it."

"Maybe he came with her. He could have planted the syringe here. Hell, for all we know she could have planted it for him."

"You think she's in on it?"

Jake grinned. "I'd love to think that, but I'm biased. I want to win the election, but I want to win it fairly. I want to get all the facts before we start pointing fingers or I could lose all credibility."

"Nita never mentioned Malcolm being here, but I'll see what I can find out." Connor leaned on the car next to him. "So, Dad was pretty mad, I guess."

"At first he was more stunned than angry. He's used to you doing whatever he asks. After we talked for a few minutes I could tell he was really getting mad. He expected me to drop what I'm doing and take over for you. When I told him no, he just about had a stroke."

"I should probably feel guilty, but I don't. The truth

is, I don't care what he thinks anymore. I don't know why I ever did." He sighed, long and deep. "That's not true. I know why I did it. Because I was jealous."

"Jealous of what?"

"Of you. You were the popular twin. The twin everyone loved. And no matter how much you screwed up, you always managed to come out ahead somehow. I've done everything our father ever asked of me, but not once have I felt like he approved of me."

Jake laid a hand on Connor's shoulder. "That's the difference between you and me. I don't give a damn what he thinks of me. I've made a lot of mistakes in my life, but I don't have too many regrets."

"When we were kids, I used to wish I could be you, just for a day, so I could know what it felt like."

Jake laughed. "You probably would have been disappointed. My life wasn't as exciting as it looked. I was as confused and mixed-up as most other kids, I just didn't let it show. The important thing now is that despite everything, I'm exactly where I'm supposed to be. How many people can say that?"

Connor looked up at Nita, realizing he felt exactly the same way. He couldn't even explain how he was sure. He only knew that he belonged here, and that whatever he'd been, whatever had happened in his past, didn't matter anymore.

"I was going to ask if you're in love with her, but I think I've already got my answer," Jake said.

"She doesn't want a relationship."

"So what are you going to do?"

"I'm going to marry her." He looked up at his brother and grinned. "She just doesn't know it yet."

* * *

Nita woke with the length of a very warm, very aroused male body curled behind her. Though she typically liked to sprawl out and hog the bed, Connor liked to spoon. The past couple of nights, she'd begun to grow used to him sleeping with her. Not that he'd given her a choice, considering, once he was in her bed, he wouldn't leave. Every time she made noise like he should get up and go to his own room, he would start kissing her and touching her and she would forget what she was saying, until he had her so completely exhausted and sexually sated, she didn't care where he slept. And yeah, okay, she kind of liked waking in his arms, and he didn't seem to care that she climbed out of bed looking like Frankenstein's bride.

She liked watching him while he slept, too. The lines of his face softened and he looked younger. She also liked the way he woke her—with his hands and his mouth in all the places she loved to feel them. Red-hot sex was definitely the best way to start the morning.

The truth was, there wasn't too much she didn't like about sleeping with Connor. Which was all the more reason to put an end to it as soon as possible. She usually thought with her head, but now her heart was starting to dictate the rules and that scared her.

And she didn't scare easily.

She glanced over at the clock, saw that the alarm was set to go off in twenty minutes, and decided she might as well get out of bed. If she waited for the alarm, Connor would wake up and start doing his magic and they wouldn't get a thing done before lunch.

She rolled out of bed, shivering as her bare feet hit the

cold wood floor. She grabbed the afghan from the foot of the bed and wrapped it around herself then walked over to the window to see what the day would be like— half hoping for torrential rain so she and Connor would have to stay indoors. She pushed the curtains aside and peered out. The sun glowed pink across the horizon and a fine mist of dew covered the ground. Another beautiful day—oh well. Then she looked down at the driveway and saw that the second truck was parked there.

Five days after her daddy had left, he was finally home. He'd called Saturday and left a message saying he would be gone for a few days, but when he did come home, he and Nita were going to have a talk—meaning she'd been found out. Considering Jane's car was nowhere to be seen, Nita's fib obviously hadn't done any good. She'd been worried sick that something horrible had happened, or that her meddling had only made things worse. What if, instead of going to see Jane, he'd gone to see Lucas Devlin and they'd duked it out?

She must have left a dozen messages on her daddy's voice mail, but he hadn't called her back. She'd even tried calling Jane to see if she'd heard from him, but kept getting her answering machine. Jane either wasn't there, or was too mad to call her back.

Now that Will was home, he was going to get a piece of Nita's mind.

"Is he home?"

Nita turned to see Connor sitting up in bed, stretching. She loved the way he looked in the morning, all rumpled and sexy. And he felt even better. "How did you know?"

"I heard the truck pull in late last night."

"You should have woken me."

"I tried. You were out cold." He pulled the covers back, patting the bed beside him. "It's early, come back to bed."

"The alarm is set to go off in less than fifteen minutes. I should get ready for work."

"You sure? You'd be amazed what I can do in fifteen minutes."

She could think of a dozen reasons not to get back into bed, but her feet carried her there regardless. Another prime example of her heart not listening to her head.

"Okay, but only fifteen minutes." She let the afghan slide to the floor and climbed in beside him. Then his hands were on her body, driving her crazy like no one ever had before.

This was too good she realized, too perfect. And she knew it had to end.

Later, she decided, as his hot mouth found her nipple. She would worry about it later.

An hour and a half later Nita headed down the stairs, showered and dressed, ready to have it out with her father. Maybe what she'd done was a little unethical, telling him Jane was in cahoots with a Devlin, but what he'd done was far worse. A man couldn't just disappear for five whole days and not worry his family sick.

She stomped her way to his bedroom and pounded on the door. "Daddy, I want to talk to you."

Through the door she heard the covers rustling, the sound of hushed voices. She couldn't believe it. He had someone in there! Had he been so distraught he'd picked up some floosy? Had Nita driven him to it?

She didn't know who to be more angry at, him or herself.

The door opened a crack and her daddy stood there in his robe. "Now isn't a good time to talk."

Well, that was just too damned bad, because she had something to say. "Have you got a woman in there?"

He looked more exasperated than angry. "If you must know, yes, I do."

Nita's mouth fell open.

"Don't look at me like that. I made it legal first." He wiggled his hand in front of her face, showing off a shiny new wedding band. "We got hitched in Vegas."

She was almost too stunned to form words, but somehow she managed. "You're *married?*"

"Yep."

This was even worse than she'd thought. They were never going to get Jane back now. And she doubted any wife he picked up in Vegas would know how to run a farm.

"How do you think Jane is going to feel about this?"

"Lemme ask her." He called over his shoulder, "Jane, honey, how do you feel about me getting hitched?"

"I'd say it's about time," Jane called back.

This time Nita was too stunned to speak.

"Satisfied?" her daddy asked and Nita nodded numbly. "Then if you don't mind, I'm going to get back to my bride. I'm a newlywed, you know."

The door snapped shut and Nita stood there a good five minutes, letting it all sink in. Her plan had worked. She'd gotten Jane and her daddy back together, just as she'd hoped to. She'd never seen him look so happy and she knew Jane had to be feeling like the luckiest woman alive. It's all Nita had ever wanted for the both of them, so why did she feel so jumbled up inside?

She was happy and excited and something else, something darker.

Then she realized she was jealous. Nita was used to having her daddy all to herself. Now that he was a husband, she would have to share him. What was even worse, though it shamed her to feel this way, she was jealous of their happiness. Jane would be the perfect wife—everything Nita would never be.

Nita had been this way long enough to know she would never change, even if she tried. But for the first time in her life, deep down, she wished she were different. She wished she could find a man to love her for exactly who she was, someone to start a family with, to spend her life with. At that moment she wanted it so bad it was a sharp ache in her chest.

And she wanted the man to be Connor.

Somewhere in the past few weeks, she'd gone and done the one thing she'd promised she would never do. She'd let herself fall in love. And she suspected, from the way he looked at her, the way he touched her, maybe he was falling in love with her, too.

Nothing could be worse.

No matter how much she ached for it, she knew it would never work. Men expected certain things from the women they married. They wanted someone to cook and clean and take care of them. Things that she couldn't do. Couldn't and wouldn't, because she refused to end up like her momma—so unhappy it killed her. She could never be a proper wife, and that was what Connor deserved.

There was no way around it, she had to end this thing between herself and Connor, and she had to do it soon.

Maybe this morning, before they got in deeper than they already were.

With a heavy heart, she walked to the kitchen and started fixing a pot of coffee. A few minutes later, when she heard footsteps behind her, she knew it was Connor, and she knew what she had to do.

"So, did you talk to him?"

"Yeah, I talked to him." You can do this, she told herself. It'll be easy. Just flat out tell him it's over.

She forced herself to turn and look at him. He was dressed in jeans and a flannel shirt, his hair still damp from his shower, his chin cleanly shaved. He looked so good she wanted to cry, and the ache in her chest throbbed even harder. She was so nervous her hands were trembling.

Nothing about this was going to be easy.

"Was he mad that you lied about Jane working for the Devlins?"

"Actually, it never came up. He was too busy telling me how he and Jane ran off to Vegas and got hitched."

"No kidding. That's good news, right?"

"Yeah, it's real good." Just do it. Tell him.

"How come you don't sound happy?" There was so much genuine concern in his eyes, she couldn't stand to look at him a second longer.

She turned and busied herself with putting the coffee can back in the cupboard. "I am happy for them, I guess it'll just take a little getting used to."

Say it now, she coaxed, when you're not looking at him. Then Connor's arms wrapped around her from behind, drawing her against his solid chest. "It's okay to be confused, or even a little upset," he said.

That's when she knew it was hopeless. She could never do it with him holding her this way, with him being so sweet and understanding.

She turned in his arms and buried her face against his shirt, so he wouldn't see the tears welling in her eyes. Maybe just coming right out and telling him wasn't the way to go, not if she couldn't force the words out. She didn't even know what to say.

There had to be another way to do this.

She held on tight, wishing she never had to let go.

"Hey, you all right?" he asked, stroking her back.

"I'm all right," she choked out, her tears pushing closer the surface. "Just a little emotional. Must be PMS."

"Maybe I ought to take you back upstairs and see if I can't make you feel better," he said.

He tucked his finger under her chin, lifting her face, then he kissed her—so slow and sweet she knew she couldn't tell him no.

One more day, she decided. One more day and she'd figure out a way to put an end to this once and for all.

Fourteen

Connor watched from the fence as Nita worked with Buttercup in the training pen, wondering what was going on in her head, what she was thinking.

She looked the same, sounded the same, even acted the same at times, but in the week since her father and Jane had returned, something had changed. At first Connor had written it off as her reaction to her father's marriage, but he didn't think that was it.

He couldn't even put his finger on what it was exactly that was different. There were times when she would look at him, but he didn't think she was really seeing him. It was as if her mind was somewhere else, working something through. Other times she looked at him so intensely it was as though she were trying to communicate without actually talking to him.

Even her temperament seemed to have changed. Most of the time she ran hot or cold. Either she was hopping mad at him or, tearing his clothes off. Sex was different, too. The first few times, even though it was fantastic, she'd had a casual, almost flippant air about her. Lately she'd been putting her heart and soul into it and, though it could have been a trick of the light, sometimes he could swear she had tears in her eyes. She'd given up trying to kick him out of bed at night, too, and slept curled up tight in his arms.

He knew that if they weren't careful, someone was going to catch them in a compromising position. He was pretty sure Jane had figured it out as soon as she'd come home, but so far she hadn't told Will. If she had, Connor would have heard about it. At some point, he was going to have to have a talk with Will so he could make his intensions clear.

First he'd like to know what was going on in that head of Nita's. Every time he tried to talk to her about it, she'd start kissing him and taking his clothes off, making it impossible to concentrate on a damned thing. It was just a feeling, but he suspected she had something up her sleeve, and it wasn't going to be good.

"She looks good," he said, as Nita led Buttercup to the gate.

"She'll be ready to go home soon," Nita said. "Probably Monday."

"You'll miss her."

She rubbed the horse's neck. "Yeah, she's a real gem."

"If you're finished for the afternoon, I thought maybe you and I could take a ride out along the fence line."

"Why, did the boys see someone out there last night?"

"Nope. Just got a feeling." The truth was, there hadn't been any disturbances lately. Whoever it was had either given up, or was waiting for the opportune time to strike again. Meaning he had to constantly be on his guard. They had determined that Malcolm had never been to the farm with Gretchen, not that it discounted him as a suspect. The club was keeping an eye on him just in case.

The real reason Connor wanted Nita out there with him, was so that they could talk. She wouldn't be able to use her charms to distract him if she was sitting on a horse.

"Nita," Jimmy called from the bunkhouse. "You got a minute?"

Nita handed Buttercup's reins to Connor. "Take her in the stable and saddle Goliath up."

He led Buttercup to the stable as she jogged off to talk to Jimmy. Maybe now he would get some answers from her.

He'd saddled Goliath, and was getting ready to go find Nita when she walked into the stable, shutting the door behind her. "I've almost got them…"

He trailed off when he looked at Nita, saw the fire in her eyes, the way she was slowly undoing the buttons on her shirt as she walked toward him.

Aw, hell, not again.

"I changed my mind," Nita said. "I don't want to go riding."

He didn't have to ask what she did want to do. That was pretty clear when she tossed her shirt to the floor then braced her hands on his chest and pushed him against the back wall. She started to unfasten his belt, but he grabbed her hands.

"Someone could walk in and catch us."

She pulled her hands free and cupped the crotch of his jeans. "I guess we'll just have to make it a quick one."

He was about to object, then she started kissing him, and as usual, the rational part of his brain temporarily went AWOL. He was ready to give her whatever she wanted, when he had the sudden sensation they were being watched, then heard someone clear his throat. He opened his eyes to find Will standing in the stable doorway, shaking his head.

Nita spun around and covered herself with her arms. Thankfully Connor hadn't gotten as far as removing her bra.

"Um, hi, Daddy."

She didn't seem too surprised to see him, and Connor got the distinct feeling this was no accident.

"I came out to tell you that I just talked to your sister and she's coming home for a while." Will sighed, shaking his head. "Girl, you are gonna be the death of me."

"Sir, this is my fault," Connor said.

"I doubt that," Will said. He looked more resigned than angry. "Do I need to go get my shotgun?"

"No, Daddy." Nita bent down and picked up her shirt, holding it against her. "Connor will leave."

"I'm not going anywhere," Connor said.

Nita turned to him. "I know you feel we need protection, but surely the Cattleman's Club could send someone else."

"No, they can't," Connor said.

She turned back to her father. "He'll leave, Daddy."

"No, I won't. And my being here has nothing to do with protecting you."

Now Will looked intrigued. "If that's true, then why are you here?

Since she was so gun-shy Connor had wanted to wait awhile, till the time was right, let her get used to the idea slowly. Too late for that now. "I've been planning to have a talk with you. I guess now is as good a time as any. I love your daughter, and I have every intention of marrying her."

"*Marrying* me?" Nita spun to face him, a look of horror on her face. "You have got to be joking."

"No joke."

"Well, you have my blessing," Will said.

Nita shot back around. "Daddy! Don't encourage him!"

As if he needed encouraging. And he could see this was going to be a bit tougher than he expected. "Will, could I have a word alone with your daughter?"

"Sure," Will said. "And good luck. You're gonna need it."

Didn't Connor know it. But this time he was getting what he wanted. What she wanted too, even if she wouldn't admit it.

When Will was gone, Connor turned to Nita. "Is this how you got rid of the others?"

She yanked on her shirt. "What others?"

"The other men. When they start to get too close you set up a confrontation with your father so he can chase them off? Because I know it was no accident he happened to walk into the stable. You knew he was coming. That's why you threw yourself at me."

She didn't say a word, just gave him a death glare.

"It would have made for a tidy little end to this affair, wouldn't it? And you thought I'd take off with my tail between my legs."

"Which I can see you're not going to do. And who the hell ever said *anything* about marriage?"

"Me. Just now."

"You don't want to marry me."

"I believe I just said I do."

She buttoned her shirt. "Well, maybe I don't want to marry you. You ever think of that?"

"Not really."

"Well, you should have, because I don't! I don't *ever* want to get married."

She was trying to act tough, but he could see she was conflicted. He wasn't sure why she was fighting this so hard, but he had a feeling he was about to find out. "So, all this time you've just been using me for sex?"

"Pretty much, yeah. I thought we established that a couple of weeks ago, when I told you I don't do relationships." She spun around and stomped toward the door, tucking her shirt into her jeans.

Connor followed her. "You're outta luck, Nita. Because I don't want this to end, and I don't think you do, either."

"No, you're outta luck, cowboy. I *do* want this to end." She shoved her way out the door into the bright sunshine.

He was right behind her. He'd never physically chased a woman before, but he supposed there was a first for everything. "Is it because you don't love me?"

She stopped and turned to him. "No."

Jimmy stood outside the stable with Nita's father and two of the hands. They all turned to look at him and Nita. He preferred not to do this with an audience, but if she wanted it that way, fine.

"So you *do* love me," Connor said.

She frowned and the tough facade slipped just a little. "I didn't say that."

"So which is it? You love me or you don't."

She glanced over at the men, then back at Connor. "It doesn't matter either way, because I would make a lousy wife."

"How do you figure?"

"You've lived here a month, what do you think? I can't cook, I hate to clean. I can't even run a damned washing machine!"

"Yeah? What's your point?"

She looked at him as if he was nuts. "That *is* my point. I'm just not wife material."

"By whose standards?"

That one gave her pause. She didn't seem to know how to answer.

"What did you think? That once we were married I would expect you to throw on an apron and turn into Jane? I fell in love with *you,* Nita, just the way you are. I don't want to change a thing."

She didn't look convinced. "You say that now, but things change."

"That's one thing that won't. Ever. You have my word." He put his hands on her shoulders. "Now, I'm going to ask you again, do you love me or not?"

"Yeah, Nita. Do you love him or not," one of the hands called.

Jimmy whacked him hard on the back of the head and said, "Let the lovebirds talk."

Nita shot Jimmy a nasty look. "We are not *lovebirds.*"

"So you don't love him?" her father asked.

"Of course I do!" she huffed out.

Connor had known in his heart, but it was a relief to hear her admit it out loud. He pulled her against his chest and wrapped his arms around her and they were encouraged with a round of applause.

"I love you, Connor," she said softly. "And I want to be with you, but I can't."

He held her tight, knowing without a doubt, this is exactly where she belonged. "Give me one good reason."

"This farm, my family—it's my life. I can't leave. I don't *want* to."

"And I would never ask you to. If it's what you want, and it's okay with your father, we could live right here."

"I told you before," Will said. "This is your home now, Connor. You two stay as long as you like."

"What will *you* do?" Nita asked Connor.

"Exactly what I've been doing for the past month. Working on the farm."

She shook her head, looked up at him. "That's not fair to you. You need to do what you want to do or you'll regret it the rest of your life."

"Nita, this *is* what I want to do."

"Really?"

"But I don't want to be your employee forever. I'd like to be your partner."

"Partner?"

"With capital, I think you could expand your business. And I have lots of money just waiting to be spent. I can't think of a better way."

"Sure would be nice to see this place back on it's feet again," Jimmy said, and Will nodded his agreement.

"And suppose you get tired of it?" Nita asked. "What then?"

"There's no law saying that I can't change my mind later and do something else. Become a silent partner. Whatever you and you father are comfortable with."

She gazed up at him, an almost dreamy look in her eyes. "There are so many things I've wanted to do with the farm but we just haven't had the money...."

"Now you'll have it. We'll make this the most successful horse farm in West Texas."

She narrowed her eyes at him. "What about babies?"

"No more than seven or eight," he teased.

"That's not funny."

"How about one or two—three tops."

"If I marry you, people in town will think I'm a sell-out," she said. "They'll think I compromised my beliefs and caved to their influence."

Connor grinned. "Well, there's a really dumb reason not to get married."

She smiled, too. "Yeah, I guess it is. You promise you won't ever expect me to learn to cook."

"Yeah, I promise. I value my life too much."

She gave him a playful poke. "You won't make me have a big wedding will you?"

"Not if you don't want one. We could do what your father and Jane did and drive to Vegas, or we could find a judge. Whatever you want."

She shook her head. "You're serious about this? You really want to marry me?"

Connor laughed. "Yes Nita, I really want to marry you. I'll say it a thousand times if that'll convince you."

"I'm convinced," Will said, but Nita didn't seem to hear him.

Her eyes were fixed skeptically on Connor, as though she still didn't think it could be true. "You want all of it. The marriage, the partnership—everything?"

"In my whole life, this is the first thing I am one hundred percent sure about. I want it all, and I want it with you."

She wrapped her arms around his neck, and a wide grin curled her mouth. "Then, cowboy, I am all yours."

* * * * *

If you enjoyed what you just read,
then we've got an offer you can't resist!

Take 2 bestselling love stories FREE!

Plus get a FREE surprise gift!

Clip this page and mail it to Silhouette Reader Service™

IN U.S.A.
3010 Walden Ave.
P.O. Box 1867
Buffalo, N.Y. 14240-1867

IN CANADA
P.O. Box 609
Fort Erie, Ontario
L2A 5X3

YES! Please send me 2 free Silhouette Desire® novels and my free surprise gift. After receiving them, if I don't wish to receive anymore, I can return the shipping statement marked cancel. If I don't cancel, I will receive 6 brand-new novels every month, before they're available in stores! In the U.S.A., bill me at the bargain price of $3.80 plus 25¢ shipping and handling per book and applicable sales tax, if any*. In Canada, bill me at the bargain price of $4.47 plus 25¢ shipping and handling per book and applicable taxes**. That's the complete price and a savings of at least 10% off the cover prices—what a great deal! I understand that accepting the 2 free books and gift places me under no obligation ever to buy any books. I can always return a shipment and cancel at any time. Even if I never buy another book from Silhouette, the 2 free books and gift are mine to keep forever.

225 SDN DZ9F
326 SDN DZ9G

Name	(PLEASE PRINT)	
Address	Apt.#	
City	State/Prov.	Zip/Postal Code

Not valid to current Silhouette Desire® subscribers.

Want to try two free books from another series?
Call 1-800-873-8635 or visit www.morefreebooks.com.

* Terms and prices subject to change without notice. Sales tax applicable in N.Y.
** Canadian residents will be charged applicable provincial taxes and GST.
  All orders subject to approval. Offer limited to one per household.
  ® are registered trademarks owned and used by the trademark owner and or its licensee.

DES04R   ©2004 Harlequin Enterprises Limited

eHARLEQUIN.com

The Ultimate Destination for Women's Fiction

For FREE online reading, visit
www.eHarlequin.com now and enjoy:

Online Reads
Read **Daily** and **Weekly** chapters from
our Internet-exclusive stories by your
favorite authors.

Interactive Novels
Cast your vote to help decide how these
stories unfold…then stay tuned!

Quick Reads
For shorter romantic reads, try our
collection of Poems, Toasts, & More!

Online Read Library
Miss one of our online reads?
Come here to catch up!

Reading Groups
Discuss, share and rave with other
community members!

For great reading online,
visit www.eHarlequin.com today!

A violent storm.

A warm cabin.

One bed...for two strangers
stranded overnight.

Author

Bronwyn Jameson's

latest PRINCES OF THE OUTBACK novel
will sweep you off your feet and into
a world of privilege and passion!

Don't miss

The Ruthless Groom

Silhouette Desire #1691
Available November 2005

Only from Silhouette Books!

**Coming in November
from Silhouette Desire**

DYNASTIES : THE ASHTONS

*A family built on lies…brought together
by dark, passionate secrets*

continues with

SAVOR THE SEDUCTION

by Laura Wright

Grant Ashton came
to Napa Valley to discover the truth
about his family…but found so much
more. Was Anna Sheridan, a woman
battling her own demons, the answer
to all Grant's desires?

*Available this November wherever
Silhouette books are sold.*

COMING NEXT MONTH

#1687 SAVOR THE SEDUCTION—Laura Wright
Dynasties: The Ashtons
Scandals had rocked his family but only one woman was able to shake him to the core.

#1688 BOSS MAN—Diana Palmer
Long, Tall Texans
This tough-as-leather attorney never looked twice at his dedicated assistant…until now!

#1689 HIGHLY COMPROMISED POSITION—Sara Orwig
Texas Cattleman's Club: The Secret Diary
How could she have known the sexy stranger who fathered her child was her family's sworn enemy?

#1690 THE CHASE IS ON—Brenda Jackson
The Westmorelands
His lovely new neighbor was a sweet temptation this confirmed bachelor couldn't resist.

#1691 THE RUTHLESS GROOM—Bronwyn Jameson
Princes of the Outback
She delivered the news that his bride-to-be had run away…never expecting to be next on his "to wed" list.

#1692 MISTLETOE MANEUVERS—Margaret Alison
Mixing business with pleasure could only lead to a hostile takeover…and a whole lot of passion.

SDCNM1005